SECRET HEARTACHE

Midwife Emma Finch starts work at a new hospital, the Bob, back in her native Yorkshire. It's supposed to be a fresh start for her and her daughter, Keira, but then she discovers that Nick Logan — the man she once loved with all her heart, and who left her when she needed him most — is her department consultant. It soon becomes clear that the old spark between them is still very much alive. Can Emma and Nick reforge a relationship after the heartbreak of the past five years?

TERESA ASHBY

◆

SECRET HEARTACHE

Complete and Unabridged

LINFORD
Leicester

First published in Great Britain in 2014

First Linford Edition
published 2015

A catalogue record for this book is available
from the British Library.

ISBN 978–1–4448–2620–3

Published by
F. A. Thorpe (Publishing)
Anstey, Leicestershire

Set by Words & Graphics Ltd.
Anstey, Leicestershire
Printed and bound in Great Britain by
T. J. International Ltd., Padstow, Cornwall

This book is printed on acid-free paper

1

This wasn't happening. It couldn't be. Emma watched the midwife's face as the ultrasound image appeared on screen and saw her mouth droop and the colour drain from her face.

'I'm going to get Mr Smith,' she said, eyes still on the screen. 'He should see this.'

'What's happening?' Emma said, struggling to stay calm. 'Will someone please tell me?'

Her pleas fell on deaf ears. One of the younger nurses present squeezed her shoulder. 'Nothing to worry about,' she murmured, but her words brought no comfort and nor did the tone of her voice. Clearly there was something to worry about, and no one knew that more than Emma. She struggled to sit up, but firm hands held her still.

'One of the babies isn't doing quite

as well as she should,' someone else said and then the room was suddenly full of people. Who were they all? Emma looked round in fear and despair. She saw some faces she recognised, some she didn't. Most of them didn't belong there, but she didn't understand why.

'What does that mean?' Emma cried, although she knew perfectly well what it meant. She ought to. She was a midwife herself, but she'd never experienced anything like this before. Everyone appeared to be falling apart around her and no one seemed to have a clue what to do. She found herself at the centre of a sea of worried faces.

If Nick were here . . .

She shut her eyes tight. Nick couldn't be here. Nick was in Australia. He didn't know anything about this pregnancy and it was too late now to inform him. But what would he say if he knew? What would he do? She bit down hard on her lip and tasted blood. She wanted him here, so very much.

'Are you in pain?' the midwife was back and bending over the bed looking at her.

'Just scared. Tell me, please, what's going on?'

'Mr Smith is on his way. He will explain things to you.'

'Explain what?' Emma cried. 'Has something happened? Has there been a change? Stop patronising me and tell me! I have to know what's going on with my babies. They were both doing so well. What's changed?'

She knew the risks of carrying monoamniotic twins: two babies sharing one sac but with two separate cords; the possibility of the intertwined cords becoming compressed, which could prove fatal for one or both babies. She knew all that, but that was why she was in hospital for bed rest, so that the babies could be monitored and action taken at once if necessary.

Placing her hands on her stomach, the gel cool against her hot hands, she willed her babies to be all right. So far they had been. Everyone was hopeful, and no one more so than Emma.

'Emma,' the midwife said softly, 'one of your babies isn't doing so well. Her heartbeat is erratic and I think Mr Smith will decide that we shouldn't wait any longer for that C-section.'

It's too soon! The words jumped into Emma's mind. How many times had she heard that from a frightened mother-to-be? Too soon. And how many times had she calmly reassured them that yes, it was a little early, but that the baby stood a very good chance of survival? How different it felt to be on the receiving end. They were just words.

'I'm only thirty-one weeks,' Emma said. 'I'm still in the danger zone for the worst of the preemie problems.'

Mr Smith, the obstetrician entered the room, checked the screen then smiled down at Emma. She forced a smile in return, but the sides of her mouth shook and she had to bite back tears.

'I don't think we can put this off any longer, Emma,' he said with quiet

4

authority. 'I'm going to go ahead with the C-section, a little earlier than we would have liked, but we have no choice. Is there anyone you'd like us to call?'

'Nick,' she choked. 'Oh, Nick.'

He should be here, holding her hand, helping to bring these two early little lives into the world. But he didn't even know they'd started this perilous journey. And now his babies might live and die in the space of a few minutes and he would never know.

'Nick?' the midwife said with a frown as she flicked through the sheets of paper in her hands.

'Aunt Rose,' Emma amended, coming to her senses. It was no use her calling out Nick's name, because he wasn't here to hear her. 'Aunt Rose said she'd come.'

'I know we would have preferred to wait longer, Emma,' Mr Smith said kindly. 'But I'm afraid it's our only option.'

In the next moment, Emma was being pushed to theatre, doors opening as they swept along as if the doors themselves understood the urgency of the situation. It really was a matter of life and death. She stared up at the ceiling, picking out cracks and blemishes in the paint, counting the pipes that ran overhead. So many pipes. She'd never really noticed before. What were they all for? She flooded her mind with trivialities because she didn't want to think about what was happening.

Rose was ushered in, her mouth covered with a mask, her small frame drowned by a gown, her eyes wide and anxious as she hurried over to stand beside Emma. Her red curls cascaded out around the cap on her head. No one had told her to tuck them away. Emma gripped her hand and Rose gently cupped her other hand over the top of Emma's. How had she got here so quickly all the way from Yorkshire? She wasn't supposed to be coming down until nearer Emma's due date. But Rose had always been there when Emma needed her. No one else ever had.

'Thank you so much for coming,' she whispered as a tear slid down her cheek. 'I didn't want to do this alone.'

'Oh, love,' Rose said, her own eyes welling up. 'I was here anyway. I was on my way in to see you when they diverted me here.'

'Are you sure you're all right with all this?' Emma said and felt her aunt's grip on her hand tighten.

'Of course I am,' Rose said, but her eyes were awash with trepidation and Emma knew that it took every ounce of her courage for her aunt to be with her. She couldn't even watch minor procedures on the television without feeling ill. 'Don't worry about me. I'm here for you, Emma, you and the babies.'

'The babies will be all, right won't they?' Emma whimpered, and her voice was small and weak and afraid — not her voice at all. All this time she'd been reassuring Rose that there was nothing to worry about, and now finally she was sharing the worries.

'Of course they will, my darling,'

Aunt Rose said and because she had said it, it must be true. 'Sh, now, it will soon be over.'

Emma gulped back her fear. It was like a blockage in her throat, choking her. She'd carried these babies so carefully these past few months, taking care about what she did, what she ate, what she thought. You were supposed to think beautiful thoughts and that was exactly what she'd done.

But now her thoughts were dark and anxious and filled with foreboding, and the hope she'd carried in her heart was quickly fading.

If only she had found out about the pregnancy before she and Nick split up. He would have been here with her, would have made everything all right. But if he had been forced to change his plans because of the pregnancy, wouldn't he think she'd done it on purpose? Wouldn't he feel trapped? Resentful? Her mind reeled and time blurred.

'Here we go, this one's an eager beaver,' Mr Smith said jovially. 'Baby number one is home free.'

There was a sudden flurry of activity as the first baby was wrapped in a green cloth and taken immediately by the neonatal staff who were on standby. Emma saw all this from a different perspective to usual; saw it from the eyes of a terrified mother in a series of snatched glimpses.

The baby was protesting. It wasn't a strong cry, but it was a determined one. Emma's heart ached to hold her, comfort her. *My baby*, she thought, *don't give up*.

'Just a quick look,' someone said, showing her the tiny bundle.

'Oh,' Rose gasped. 'Did you see her, Emma? Did you see her? She's so tiny — like a little baby bird fallen out of the nest.'

Emma couldn't speak. One baby, safe. Eyes tight shut, not looking at this big new world into which she'd just been born; touched briefly on the cheek by her mother before being whisked away.

'Keira,' Emma whispered. 'Her name is Keira Rose.'

It was what she'd decided for the first born. And by giving her a name, making her real, she felt she'd ensured her survival.

But as the joy of seeing her baby, alive and safe swelled inside her, something else penetrated her euphoria, smashing it to pieces like a dropped vase on a hard floor. Happiness was such a fragile thing; it could be taken away in the blink of an eye.

'Come on, Miss Finch, you can't stay tucked up in there any longer. It's time to leave, my dear,' Mr Smith murmured, speaking to the remaining baby. He was an older man, very capable, very experienced, and he sounded very much in control — but was there an edge to that voice? Was Emma imagining things, or had real concern slipped in?

He fell silent then, too busy to speak. A hush had fallen over the whole room. The time seemed to go on and on. Emma looked up at Rose, who was watching the doctor. C-sections didn't usually take as long as this. Emma was aware of time slipping by, precious seconds turning into crucial minutes.

Keira Rose had been whisked away to the NICU before Emma had even had a chance to hold her.

'The cord is around the baby's neck,' Rose whispered, knowing that Emma needed to know what was happening. 'The doctor is trying to get the baby out, but she's hiding.'

Hiding? It seemed such a silly thing to say that Emma laughed, and it turned immediately to a sob. She had to stay calm. Had to keep it together. And she knew what Rose meant. Sometimes babies could bury themselves, and with the added danger of the cord compressing, it could make things incredibly dangerous.

I don't want my baby to be in danger, Emma thought silently. *I want her to be safe and real and alive.* Tears slid down her face and pooled around her ears.

The doctor was struggling, fighting

almost. Fighting to save the second baby. He was sweating. Then at last there was movement, after so many long minutes. 'I have her foot,' Mr Smith said triumphantly, and then the baby was free of the womb which had become a deadly prison.

There was no cry. No sound at all.

Come on, Emma thought. *Come on. Sweet, precious, darling child, please make a sound. Please live.* She saw someone from the neonatal team take the second baby away.

'She's having major difficulty breathing,' Mr Smith said to Emma in such a matter-of-fact manner that you might think it was no problem at all. 'But not to worry.'

'Her name is Daisy,' Emma called out. 'Is she all right?'

Emma strained to hear what was being said and heard only 'Severe respiratory distress' before Daisy was rushed from the room.

'What's happening?' Emma whispered. They hadn't shown this baby to her. They'd taken her straight away. 'Where's my baby? Is she going to be all right?'

And then those words. 'We're doing everything we can. Try not to worry.'

There were faces, so many of them, all looking at her. Emma struggled to get away. She had to get up, save her baby. Then Nick's face loomed into view. He was standing over to one side, arms folded across his chest, wearing faded blue scrubs with a mask dangling round his neck.

'When exactly did you take it upon yourself to keep all this to yourself? What gave you the right to deny the father of these children his opportunity to say goodbye?'

'You are their father and no one is saying goodbye,' Emma cried. It was too painful. The birth, the danger, and now Nick's anger. 'They're going to live — both of them this time! I won't let her go, I won't let her go!'

'Too late,' Nick said, his voice bitter. 'You failed, Emma.'

'No!' Emma thrashed from side to side in the bed, trying to escape. 'She's not dead yet. Daisy's not dead. You've got to give her a chance.'

'I could have saved her, Emma,' Nick said, his voice harsh. 'Why didn't you give me a chance? Why didn't you tell me?'

'I'm sorry, so sorry, but I didn't know where to find you. Please forgive me, please.'

Somewhere in the haze, she knew she must be dreaming. No, not dreaming; reliving a nightmare into which she'd added more over the years. Nick hadn't been part of the original nightmare. He knew nothing of any of this. Rose hadn't been there either. Emma had faced it alone, but some inner defence mechanism put Rose into the dream, gave her someone to cling to, someone who understood. If it wasn't for Rose's hand holding hers in her dream, she didn't know what she would do.

Facing all of that alone had been so hard. In actual fact it had been a young nurse who had held her hand, and she had been the one trying to reassure Emma during the C-section, but it wasn't the same as having someone there you knew; someone who loved you.

Every time this happened she wanted to make the ending different; tried to make it so that Daisy was all right.

'Emma. Emma, love, it's all right,' Aunt Rose said, but hers was the only calm voice among all those others all clamouring to be heard, and she gripped her aunt's hand. She didn't want her to leave. The others could go — even Nick, because she couldn't handle his anger — but not Aunt Rose.

'Make them go away,' she whimpered. 'I can't stand his anger. He must hate me.'

'Make who go away, sweetheart?' Aunt Rose asked gently. 'There's just us here.'

Emma's eyes flickered open. Sun streamed in through the window, but that wasn't possible. There were no windows in here. And why was there no sound from the machines, no rustle of theatre gowns, no soft footfall on hard floor, no baby's cry?

Because it's a dream, Emma's consciousness told her. But irrational from sleep, she didn't want to believe it. She wanted to hang on, just in case Daisy lived this time and she could bring her back to this world with her.

Emma sat up, grasping Rose's hand tighter than ever. What was Rose doing here? She lived in the cottage next door. But how had she come out of the dream? Emma's face was soaked, her pillow drenched with tears. Her whole body felt damp and sticky with sweat as she tried to make sense of her confusion.

'Keira?'

'Still sleeping,' Rose said. 'I was hanging my washing out when I heard you call out. I thought something must be wrong and let myself in with the spare key. Was it the nightmare again? It's been so long since you had one.'

16

'Oh, God.' Emma felt her whole body sag, but she was trembling all over and her heart ached for the child she'd lost. The grief and pain were as acute as they had been almost five years ago, and the hollow place inside her yawned agonisingly.

Her eyes were open, but all she could see were those tiny twins in the NICU. She saw them in flashes, like still photographs: at first both of them were fighting, and then after a few days of so many setbacks it was becoming clear that while Keira was doing well, Daisy was weakening, slipping away despite all the efforts of the neonatal staff. Daisy just wasn't showing any signs of rallying.

'I want to hold her,' Emma remembered saying. It wasn't enough to be able to touch her. She knew her baby was dying and she didn't want her to die in an incubator devoid of human contact save the brush of a finger against her skin. She wanted her baby to know the love and warmth of her mother. And a part of her, a very significant part, thought that her love alone would be powerful enough to make this child live even though her rational side knew that survival was just not possible.

Seven days after Emma gave birth to Daisy, the doctor and nurses removed Daisy's breathing tube, took away all the wires and switched off the machines. They wrapped her as if she were a normal baby to be handed to her mother. Emma sat with her in her arms and waited for her life to pass. She kissed the tiny face.

'I love you, my sweet little angel,' she murmured, lips trembling around the words. She'd touched the tiny unresponsive hands, willed her to rally, to turn around, to show them that she could fight, she could win. But her struggle was in vain, hopeless, and she slipped away in Emma's embrace.

No one said that it was a blessing or for the best. No one said that Daisy was so damaged that even if she could have survived her life would have been a living agony. No one said it and even if they had, Emma wouldn't have believed them. It was her fault that Daisy had died. If she'd tried harder to contact Nick, stayed in Yorkshire near Rose, then Daisy might have stood more of a chance. If Nick had come back and Daisy had had both parents there, willing her to live, wanting her to survive . . . But Emma had denied her that, and now it was too late. Almost five years too late.

'I'll get you a cup of tea,' Rose said, pushing Emma's hair back from her soaking face. 'All this will have been brought on by anxiety. You're worrying about Keira starting school and starting your new job. I feared this would all be too much for you on the same day.'

'You're always there, Aunt Rose,' Emma said as her aunt moved towards the door. 'In my dream, you're always with me.'

Rose turned around and smiled gently. 'I would have been with you if you'd let me know what was happening,' she said, but her words were without accusation.

19

'If I'd known the peril those babies were in and what you were going through, I would have been there like a shot.'

'I know.' Emma smiled. 'I didn't want to worry you.'

'But you're back now,' Rose said, squeezing her hand. 'That's the main thing.'

* * *

'Stand still, Keira,' Emma laughed as she tried unsuccessfully for the umpteenth time to aim the camera at the little girl who simply could not be still, not even for the moment it would take for the camera to capture a shot.

The nightmare she'd woken from this morning had left her feeling headachy and dismal, but she'd put on a smile for Keira and before long it had become genuine.

'But I'm so excited, Mummy,' Keira said, her cheeks as round and rosy as apples. 'I'm going to school.' Her blonde curls tumbled about her face and Emma's breath was snatched away. Keira was such a beautiful little girl, and special in more ways than she would ever know.

'And that's why I want to take a photo,' Emma said. 'This is a very big day.'

'For both of you,' Rose said with a smile. 'I'd say your first day at the Robert Vincent Memorial Hospital was pretty big on the occasion scale. I'll take a photo of the two of you together so you'll always have a reminder of today.'

Emma handed over the camera. It was probably just as well that her aunt was taking the photo, since her own hands were shaking. As big days went, Aunt Rose was right — this one was enormous; and although it hadn't started very well, it was getting better by the minute.

They'd only moved into the village of Wiltonthorpe a few weeks ago, but already it felt like home. Keira had been to the village school for the occasional day here and there and had already made friends with some of the local children. And Rose lived next door and would always be on hand to take care of Keira when Emma was working.

There wasn't a person on earth whom Emma would have trusted more than Rose to look after Keira. She had never married or had children of her own, but she had a gift with children. She was kind and understanding and Emma adored, her and so did Keira.

It was a perfect arrangement. Emma had always longed to come home to Yorkshire and after five long years away, she felt the time was right. A new hospital, a new home and a new start. Well the home wasn't exactly new, Emma thought wryly. It was an old cottage with thick walls and small windows with beams across the ceilings and a huge Aga in the kitchen. They had one or two problems with the plumbing and a bit of damp here and there, but they were all things that could be fixed.

It was as if fate had brought them

here, with the job coming up at the same time that the cottage next door to Rose's came on the market, and at exactly the right time in their lives.

Right now they were in the small garden. Emma had longed for a garden for Keira to play in and now she had one. It was as if all her dreams and wishes had come true at once.

She shivered.

Rose noticed. 'Emma?'

'Someone walked over my grave,' she said, her smile wavering. It was when she had that thought about all her dreams and wishes coming true that it had happened. As if by even thinking such a thing she was inviting disaster to come knocking.

She shook herself and smiled broadly, then hunkered down beside Keira and put her arm around her. How was it possible to love another human being as much as this and not die from the intensity of it? As Keira turned to kiss her cheek, the camera flashed.

'Oh, that was a good one,' Rose

cried. 'Let's have some more.'

She didn't have to tell them to smile. Emma couldn't wipe the smile off her face and Keira was still giggling. Rose took photographs in quick succession, capturing the love between mother and daughter.

If Emma had known what awaited her at the Bob, as the new hospital had already been fondly christened, her smile would have been a lot less dazzling in the photographs. She would have been in a state of high anxiety. A strong sense of duty would have made her turn up, but it would have been to hand in her notice.

'Look at the time!' Emma cried. 'Come on, Keira. We don't want to be late on our first day.'

It wasn't far to walk to the village school, and it took less than five minutes after Keira had hugged Rose and kissed her all over her face. Emma saw Keira right into the classroom and helped her hang up her coat on a peg with her name above it. Then she gave her another hug. She was a slender child, smaller than most other children her age, with huge eyes that had changed from deepest blue to the prettiest grey, and fragile-looking but strong. Emma loved her so ferociously that it was a real physical pain at times.

'Love you.'

'Love you too, Mummy.'

'Have a lovely time, darling,' she said, knowing she mustn't allow her voice to crack even though she felt like crying. Going to school was such a giant leap. Keira wasn't her baby anymore; she was growing up, growing fast. And there was always the thought that Keira shouldn't be doing this alone. Emma should have been seeing two little girls inside for their first day. 'I'll see you later. Aunty Rose will pick you up this afternoon.'

No point in repeating all the warnings about not going off with strangers, waiting for Aunt Rose, being careful. She'd already done all that to death and she didn't want to make

Keira afraid by going on and on.

'Bye, Mummy,' Keira said, wrapping her skinny arms round Emma's neck and clinging to her for a moment so that Emma's senses were filled with the scent of soap and shampoo that clung to her little girl. Then Keira pulled free and was immediately called by one of the other children.

'You can sit on my table, Keira,' Suki, the other little girl, said as she took Keira's hand and the pair of them walked off without so much as a backward glance.

The teacher gave Emma a reassuring smile and a rather pointed wave and she took the hint and hurried away. Some of the other mothers were having more difficulty leaving their offspring. She should thank her lucky stars that Keira had gone in so happily.

Before coming back to Yorkshire, Emma had worked part-time at a hospital in the south and Keira had been looked after in the hospital crèche, so they were both used to goodbyes.

Who was she kidding? Keira might be all right with goodbyes, but Emma would never get used to leaving Keira, ever!

She knew she'd have to put Keira out of her mind. She had a job to do and if she didn't get a move on, she was going to be late.

It was a long drive to the hospital, but worth it to live in the picturesque village which held so many happy memories. Emma wanted Keira to have wonderful childhood memories too. She wanted her to remember playing in the beck, running through the fields and climbing trees. Most of all, she wanted her to remember being loved.

Emma's parents had been killed in an accident when she was little older than Keira. If it hadn't been for Emma's mother's sister Rose stepping in and taking her home to Wiltonthorpe, Emma would have ended up in care. Rose had changed her life.

The pale little girl from the city had grown strong and freckles suddenly dusted her cheeks. Her hair lightened under the sun, and her long limbs turned brown. The only thing that didn't change was the summer blue of her eyes.

Now, twenty-three years later, Emma was again the pale girl from the city, but she felt as if she'd come home for good and could at last settle down.

She should never have run away from Yorkshire and all she knew and loved in the first place, but she had and it had taken her five years to pluck up the courage to come back. And now she had, nothing was going to scare her away again.

2

'What did you say the new midwife was called?' Nick Logan asked. 'Emma something?'

'Emma Finch.' Val Thompson smiled up at Nick from behind the reception desk. 'She's twenty-eight and single and she's not due in until ten, so you can stop glaring at your watch.'

'I wasn't,' Nick laughed uneasily. Emma Finch. He didn't know anyone with that name, yet something about this, about her, rang alarm bells. She was the same age as Emma Tyler and had the same experience and qualifications. Not only that, but she'd worked at the same hospital as him at the same time, though he was damned if he could remember her. Yet the surname Finch was familiar, but why?

Perhaps it was Emma Tyler — perhaps she'd married. But Val said she was single. Divorced maybe? He'd never stopped hoping that Emma would come back, but knew it was a tall order after what happened. Yet the thought that Emma Finch might turn out to be Emma Tyler filled him with a mixture of dread and joy. He ran his tongue across his lips. After all this time, how wonderful would it be to see Emma again? But then he remembered the last time he saw her, and the pain in her eyes when he told her he was leaving the country.

'What about us?' she'd whispered.

'Us?' he'd repeated. He hadn't meant to sound so dismissive. What he wanted was for her to say she'd come with him. He'd expected her to be pleased, to congratulate him, and instead she was acting as if he'd turned into the worst kind of rat.

'You apply for a job in Australia and you don't even think to mention it to me until it's a done deal?' she'd said, anger shimmering in her eyes. 'If you wanted an end to this — to us, you only had to say! You didn't have to go to such extremes.'

'You don't understand,' he'd said, floundering, confused because this wasn't the reaction he'd expected. 'You could come with me.'

'Huh? As an afterthought? Just give up my life here and follow you round to the other side of the world? Oh, don't worry, Nick. I won't take you up on it. You're free. It's what you want, isn't it?'

Stunned, he hadn't answered. Angry, she hadn't hung around to wait for him to say any more.

'Fine,' he shouted after the slammed door. 'Don't let's bother even talking about this.'

But he had every intention of talking about it the next day and would have done if she hadn't disappeared. No one knew where she'd gone, and that was when it hit him just what a big mistake he'd made and how badly he'd read the situation; how little he'd really known about her.

'Anyway, while you're here, could

31

you pop in and see Jenny Saunders?' Val's voice broke into his thoughts. Not that thoughts of Emma were unusual. He didn't think of her every day, but he did think of her often and wonder where she was now, what she was doing. Was she in love?

He knew very well that he was going to be tortured by regret for the rest of his life, but he was well practised in the art of putting such regret to the back of his mind when he had work to do. Jenny Saunders was a worry, but he knew there had been no developments or Val would have been demanding immediate action.

'Yes, of course.' Nick nodded, bringing himself back into the here and now. He fixed Val with soft grey eyes. 'Still worrying, is she?'

Val nodded. Jenny had every right to worry, Nick thought as he made his way to the quiet side room where she was in bed, staring out of the window at a cloudless blue sky that reminded him of Emma's eyes. She hadn't heard him come in. Sadness seemed to radiate off her and he wished he could do more to reassure her. Thoughts of Emma faded like fog in sunshine and his heart went out to the young woman in the bed.

'Jenny.'

She turned at the sound of her name and smiled, happy to see him, but at the same time her eyes welled with tears and her lips began to tremble.

Nick didn't ask what had brought this on or what was the matter, because he already knew. Jenny was expecting monoamniotic twins, which meant the babies shared the same sac. The risk of their umbilical cords becoming entangled and the possibility of one or both cords becoming cinched was a major worry.

He strode over to the bed and sitting down beside her, took hold of her hand. He chose his words carefully, knowing how much she would read into everything he said, looking all the time for hidden meanings and more to worry about.

'Jenny, I know how frightened you

are,' he said gently. 'But believe me, we are ready to intervene at the first sign of trouble. That's why I've admitted you. We're watching you all the time.'

She turned red, teary eyes to him and his heart cramped. This should be a time of joy and celebration for every woman, not a time of fear and anxiety. He hated to see his mothers so upset. Jenny was thirty-two and this was her first pregnancy. These babies were very much wanted and she should be looking forward to their birth, not dreading their death.

'I know the odds aren't good,' she murmured.

'Depends how you look at it.' He smiled and squeezed her hand. 'You're young, healthy and fit, and the babies are giving us no cause for concern at present. You're doing everything we've asked of you and I have every intention of presenting you with two perfect healthy babies when the time comes.'

She managed a weak smile. Nick wasn't sure if he'd done a good enough job of convincing her not to spend so much time worrying. But it must be difficult when she was in bed all day, forbidden to do anything. The pile of books beside her bed was untouched. She couldn't even get interested in the television.

'Got any visitors coming in?' he asked.

'My husband will be along later,' she said. 'He'd be here all the time if he could, but he wants to save his time off for when . . . if the babies come home.'

'That's a *when*, not an *if*, Jenny,' Nick said. 'Remember that.'

She smiled at him. 'I want to believe you, Nick,' she said.

'Then do,' he said. And he was very glad her husband was spending so much time here. At times like this, a woman needed her partner by her side as much as possible. He just couldn't imagine how hellish it would be to have to go through something like this alone.

★ ★ ★

Having found a parking space, Emma ran into the hospital. It still had that brand-new plasticky smell, mingled with the smell of new flooring and the faintest hint of fresh paint. The floor was gleaming, the windows without a smear, and the whole place had an almost futuristic feel to it.

'Hi, good morning,' she called out cheerfully to the security man sitting behind his desk just inside the door.

'Good morning,' he said, smiling back.

Oh didn't this feel wonderful? Coming back to work full-time in her beloved Yorkshire and in a fantastic new hospital — what more could she ask?

She wasn't late, but she had hoped to arrive earlier than this. Outside the maternity wing, she stopped and ran her fingers through her short, ruffled blonde hair, then decided she'd have to do.

Excitement fluttered in her chest as she walked through the doors into the unit. Everyone seemed busy but not rushed, she was pleased to notice. And as she walked in, the woman behind the reception desk looked up at her and got to her feet. She smiled warmly. 'You must be Emma, our new midwife,' she said, holding out her hand. 'I'm Val Thompson, the . . . '

But Emma wasn't listening. She stared at the board behind Val which listed all the staff currently on duty. At the top of the list it said Nick Logan. Her heart slammed against her ribs. Nick! She blinked hard, but when she opened her eyes the name was still there.

But that couldn't be. Nick had told her he planned to take a position he'd been offered in Australia. It had come completely out of the blue. While she'd been quietly dreaming of marriage, children, and a cosy cottage in the countryside she adored, he'd been planning a life elsewhere, with or without her apparently.

She'd thought she'd be safe coming back to Yorkshire after five years. People move on, and she was unlikely to meet anyone she'd worked with before; and even if she did, too much time had elapsed for them to start putting two and two together. There was no danger in seeing Nick again unless you counted the fact that she was still being haunted by him, always seeing him in her dreams.

But he may well be married by now, and have children. Oh, amend that — he already had a child, except he didn't know it. She wished her heart would stop hammering. It was making it difficult to breathe.

'Are you all right?' Val asked. 'You've gone as white as a sheet.'

Further down the corridor one of the pristine white doors opened and swung shut behind a doctor who was heading her way. Emma knew who it was at once. Even if she hadn't seen his name on the board, she would have known him any-where just by the sound of his footsteps. She knew so much of the man, she even knew him without having to look at him. She swung round to face him as he walked towards her.

Run, run, run! Her heart pounded out the words, but she couldn't move even if she wanted to; even if her life had depended upon it.

The way that dark, almost black hair flopped over his forehead; the deep dimples in his cheeks; the curve of his mouth, always ready for a smile except when he was mad about something. The long easy strides taken by those muscular legs. One hundred percent Nick. He wasn't close enough for her to see the colour of his eyes yet, but she knew they'd be that same soft grey, so pale in contrast to his black lashes — Keira's eyes. Her heart continued to slam against her ribs, and she reached out to grip the edge of the desk because she really thought she might just fall down.

He was wearing a white shirt and dark grey trousers and he hadn't put on an ounce of weight.

She couldn't feel her legs. Couldn't feel anything except that mad, out-of-control pounding of her heart.

Nick. The guy who dominated her dreams, whose photographs she had kept, whom she had loved with her heart and soul, and who ultimately hadn't wanted a future with her.

She had never loved anyone the way she had loved Nick, neither before nor since. If she lived to be a hundred, she knew she would never fall in love with another man with even half the passion she had felt for him. Any second now he was going to recognise her, and then what would he think? That she'd come back to stalk him?

Run, run, run.

Her heart continued to pound wildly and it was all she could do to draw in a breath and let it out again as she watched his inexorable approach, every long stride bringing him closer. He hadn't recognised her yet and was looking at some paperwork in his hand. Last time he saw her she had long hair, but now it was cut short. *Run, run, run,* that terrified voice inside her screamed. *Run away now, while you still can. Get out of here. This is going to get way too complicated, and it's not just you anymore; there's Keira too.*

And that set off another voice deep within her — it was the voice of the mother she'd become, not the devil-may-care young person she used to be. *If you run, where will you go? It's taken you ages to find a job in Yorkshire. You run away from him, you run away from your dreams. You may have to move back down south, uproot Keira, disappoint Rose — and all because you can't handle your own feelings for a man who didn't want you. Too much is at stake here. You must stand your ground.* But how was she going to play this? Play it cool? Pretend she hardly remembered him? Or act pleased to see him? Which she undeniably was, in some perverse way.

He was almost level with her now, and his stride had shortened and slowed down almost imperceptibly, shock beginning to register on his chiselled, beautiful and so-familiar face.

His eyes narrowed and his lips tightened into a thin line. He was like a car trying to perform an emergency stop when it was far too late to avoid a collision. He reached for the end of his tie, smoothing it unconsciously between his fingers.

She wanted to step backwards, to keep as much space between them as possible, but she was frozen to the spot, barely able to think straight much less move her legs. Was he angry with her for being here? Pleased to see her? What?

She felt her knees buckle and almost went down, and she tightened her grip on the desk to steady herself. Val was trying to say something, but Emma couldn't hear above the pounding in her ears, and it didn't look as if Nick was listening either.

At last he spoke, and a smile softened the hard lines of his face that shock and surprise had left there. 'Emma! It's you,' he said, and the smile on his face was not what she expected. She thought he'd be annoyed to find her here, might even think she was here because of him, but if anything he looked genuinely delighted to see her. In fact for one brutal moment she thought he might even hug her. And then what?

'Nick, I had no idea . . . ' She cursed the husk in her voice that betrayed her shock.

'Neither did I. Well, maybe some. The name and your history,' he said, then he shook his head. 'What am I thinking? Welcome to the Bob. But what's with Emma Finch? Have you . . . I mean, are you married now?'

That smile. So warm. So friendly. So genuine. Confident, that was him. Not to be rattled. Not by a face from the past. But somehow grown up, different, more mature, less reckless. How could she tell all these things at a glance? She wasn't sure she could; it was just an impression.

Val was looking from one to the other of them. Emma glanced at her. She didn't want to be the subject of gossip.

Nick realised, and taking her arm drew her to one side. His touch was like an electric shock. He felt it too, pulling his hand away and looking at it, then at her, confusion showing for the first time in his eyes. She didn't understand any of this. He was the one who was going to work in Australia, as far away from her as he could possibly get.

What she had never really understood was why. But it was becoming clearer. Maybe it had been a lie all along, perhaps a way of trying to let her down gently. Perhaps he'd never had any intention of taking that job abroad. If that was the case, then it was unforgivable that he'd lied. And if that was true, then why did he look so happy to see her now?

'We have to talk,' he said urgently, his grey eyes burning into her as if he dare not let her out of his sight lest she should disappear. 'Come to my office, it's just down here.'

This time it was she who put out a hand and rested it on his arm, feeling the heat of his skin through the cotton. 'We don't have to do this,' she said evenly, knowing that they had to.

'I think we do,' he said, raising his eyebrows slightly at the desk.

Emma turned to look back at Val, who was watching them. What a great start. Like it or not, she was going to kick off her time here by being a mystery. Val would already have cottoned on that Nick and Emma had a past, and the speculation was going to be unbearable.

She followed Nick into an office and he closed the door behind her.

'Sit down,' he said and when she hesitated, he went on, 'Please.'

She sat, hoping he wasn't going to apologise for what happened between them. It was too late for that now. Far too much had happened since.

'Emma, you look terrific,' he said, and he was still looking at her as if he didn't quite believe his eyes. It was nice to receive the compliment, but she wasn't sure it was appropriate under the circumstances.

'I didn't know you worked here,' she said, speaking plainly and honestly. 'If I had, I can assure you I would never have applied for the job.'

'Why not?' He looked surprised and maybe even a little hurt. He was sitting on the other side of the desk now, long lean legs stretched out. 'Do you hate me that much?'

'Hate you?' she whispered. If only he knew. Nothing could be further from the truth. How could she ever hate him? She'd loved him once. Losing him had left a gaping wound in her heart, and there was no doubt she hated what he'd done, but hate him? Never. He was the father of her child. How could she hate him?

'I wouldn't blame you, Emma,' he said and he hesitated after saying her name, then repeated it as if he was savouring the sound. 'Emma . . . '

Emma looked at him, forcing herself to look at eyes which were Keira's eyes, and she ached for him because he had never known his two baby girls; never been given the chance to grieve for the one they had lost. And he'd missed out on all the joy that Keira had brought.

'I thought you were going to travel,' she said.

'I did,' he said softly. Ah, a trace of bitterness there. Had Australia not lived up to its promise? How long had he stuck it out before coming home? And why did she feel such a sense of gratification?

Her first thought when she'd confirmed her pregnancy had been to get in touch with him, tell him the truth, give him the option to get involved. But when she'd plucked up the courage to call him to tell him she was pregnant, she was told that he'd already gone. That was it. Gone. As if he couldn't wait to get away. What made it worse was that it had been Lola who had answered his phone. Lola, a beautiful young American girl. Whether she was telling the truth or not, it marked the end for Emma. If he'd gone, then it was too late. If he hadn't, then he'd moved Lola in and so it was hopeless anyway.

'Who is this?' Lola had asked.

'Doesn't matter,' Emma said, and it didn't. It just didn't matter anymore — she was on her own and had to get used to it.

'I called you,' she said now, trying to keep her voice even, trying to make out it didn't matter. 'Lola answered.'

'Lola?' He gave her a look almost as if he didn't know who she was talking about. 'Ah, Lola. She rented my house while I was away.'

'You planned to come back?'

'It's a long time ago, water under the bridge so to speak. Why did you call me?'

'Sorry?'

'You said you called and Lola answered.'

Whoops, nearly dropped herself in it there, and he seemed to be holding his breath as if expecting a particular answer. *I just called to tell you that you were going to be a father.* She could just come out with it, but then he'd want to see Keira, might want some involvement in her life, and Emma wasn't sure enough of him yet. Anyway, they'd managed perfectly well without him.

'It doesn't matter,' he said when she didn't answer. 'You haven't told me about your name. You don't wear a ring.'

'Tyler was my birth name,' she said. 'As you know, I was raised by my Aunt Rose Finch. I'm more Finch than I ever was Tyler. I wanted . . . needed a fresh start. I had to get rid of the old me.'

'Because of me?'

'Partly.'

My God, Emma thought. He flinched. He actually flinched. Did he feel guilty for the way he had behaved? He damn well should!

'That's why the name rang bells,' he said after a long pause. 'I can't believe I missed that, but she was always just Rose to me. How is your aunt?'

'She's very well,' Emma said, and then a tiny splinter of panic drove into her thoughts. What if he wanted to see

Rose? He had been very fond of her and they had always got along well.

'Still living in Wiltonthorpe?'

'Yes.' Emma's throat felt suddenly dry. She couldn't swallow. He wouldn't come to Wiltonthorpe, would he? Why would he? Their relationship was in the past. Over. Maybe not forgotten, but more than five years had passed and they'd both moved on.

'A beautiful village,' he said. 'Lovely church.'

She felt her face fill with heat, knew she would be turning red as he continued to unwittingly heap on the agony. Why mention the church? Did he know? No, of course he didn't. There was no way he could possibly know that she'd brought their baby back to Yorkshire to be laid to rest with her grandparents. *My God*, she thought, *I'm getting paranoid*.

'I should . . . ' She got to her feet and half-turned towards the door. She had to get out of this room before she suffocated; had to get away from him.

This was worse, so much worse than she'd ever imagined it would be. And different. In her dreams he had pulled her into his arms, begging her forgiveness. In her nightmares he had been angry, accusing. He had never been simply friendly or even pleased to see her.

'Yes, of course. I'm sorry, Emma. I shouldn't have kept you talking. You'll want to get on. Luckily you've joined us at a relatively quiet time, so you'll have a chance to get to know the staff and the department. I'll see you later. Perhaps we could have a coffee. The hospital has a very nice café with some tables outside on the patio. It's all very pleasant for staff and patients. We could catch up.'

'That would be lovely,' she said, almost falling over in her hurry to escape. As she left his office, she caught a glimpse of his face. He looked every bit as shattered and confused as she felt.

3

Emma hurried out of the office, walked briskly past the reception desk and went to hang up her coat. What a day this was turning out to be. First waking in a cold sweat having the past thrust at her in her dreams, and now this, the past in flesh and blood and very much part of the present.

It was so weird seeing Nick again. He looked just the same, but different in ways she couldn't even begin to fathom. He even smelled good, but then he always had. In some ways it felt as if no years had passed, and in others as if a lifetime had gone by, which in a way it had. Keira's lifetime at any rate.

He'd asked her if she was married. She hadn't asked him the same question, but she'd looked at his left hand and there was no ring on his finger — which didn't mean he wasn't married. And oh, God, so what if he was married? So what if he wasn't? What difference did any of it make now?

The real reason she'd taken her aunt's name was Keira. She didn't think it likely, but she'd always had it at the back of her mind that Nick might find out somehow about Keira and put two and two together. The best and most simple way to prevent that happening was to change her name. She didn't want him barging back into her life because he wanted a say in the life of the daughter he didn't even know existed.

What if he did that and then decided he'd had enough of playing daddy and wanted to leave again? Would he do that? Could he? He wasn't going to get the chance. And what about Australia? Had he plans to go back there?

'Oh, I don't know,' she said aloud, exasperated by her own random and thoroughly confused thoughts.

She'd come back to Yorkshire because she thought he'd gone to live abroad, and that after five years he wouldn't be coming back. How wrong she'd been.

The door opened and a tall, statuesque woman with dark hair framing an attractive, strongly featured and very smooth-skinned face walked in. 'June Carter,' she said, holding out her hand. 'We met at the interview, Emma. It's nice to see you again. Welcome. I hear you've already spoken to Nick.'

'Yes.' Emma nodded. 'There's something you should know.'

'That you and Nick have worked together before,' June cut in quickly. 'Our Val is an expert at putting two and two together and I don't have to tell you that news travels fast in a hospital. That's not a problem for you, is it?'

A problem? If only she knew.

'No problem at all,' Emma said lightly.

'Good.' June smiled. 'And how about Nick's father, John? Have you met him?'

'Yes, I have,' Emma said, a feeling of warmth trickling through her veins.

John Logan was an older version of Nick — calm, capable and good-looking. She liked him very much. 'I've worked with him, too in the past.'

'In that case you'll be pleased to know he comes in two days a week, although he's not in this week as he's on leave. He's semi-retired now. Well, let's get you properly acquainted with the unit and staff. We're pretty quiet at the moment, which is lucky,' June said, echoing Nick's words as she opened the door. 'I'll take you to the NICU too if we've time. First of all, though, I'd like you to meet Jenny. Nick admitted her for bed rest. At the moment I'd say she was our most important and worrying patient.'

'Complications?' Emma asked as she followed June along the corridor. The older woman had a brisk, purposeful walk and Emma almost had to run to keep up.

'You could say that. Jenny is expecting monoamniotic twins,' June explained as they reached the door to the side room. 'We're monitoring her very closely. I don't have to tell you the kind of risks involved in a case like this.'

Emma's chest slammed as June pushed the door open and she saw the young, anxious mother-to-be in the bed. And no sooner had the introductions been made than June's pager went and she had to dash away.

Emma felt as if she'd been parachuted into the middle of a nightmare. Maybe she was still dreaming and any minute now she'd wake up with Aunt Rose shaking her or Keira snuggling up in bed beside her.

'Hi, Jenny,' Emma forced herself to speak. 'How are you feeling?'

'Sick of everyone telling me that everything will be all right,' Jenny said tearfully. 'None of you can possibly know how I feel.'

Emma knew exactly how Jenny felt. She'd been in exactly the same position herself, forced to rest in bed, never knowing from one day to the next when she might have to have an emergency

C-section. And the worst of it was that she couldn't tell Jenny that; couldn't share her experience. She was torn between wanting to reassure her that she did know how she felt and wanting to keep her private life exactly that, private. And would it help Jenny anyway to know that Emma had lost one of her twins? She doubted it. Jenny needed to hear stories with happy endings right now. She had to have hope to cling to or else she had nothing to keep her strong.

Seeing Jenny's distress brought it all rushing back and she felt for her, she really did, right to the depths of her soul. 'I do understand, Jenny,' she said softly, then turned to look at the top of the bedside locker. 'Oh, you've plenty of books to read.' She picked up a book from the top of the pile and smiled. 'I've read this one. It's very good, isn't it?'

'Is it?' Jenny sighed bleakly.

'Yes,' Emma said enthusiastically. 'Try it. Lose yourself in the words. The time will pass quicker and it will give you a break from worrying. If you stop dwelling on your situation for a few minutes nothing will happen except you'll have a break from worry.'

Jenny looked up at her and smiled. 'Oh, I couldn't concentrate.'

'Try,' Emma said. 'Would you like me to read to you a bit? Just to get you started?'

Jenny looked amazed. 'Read to me?' She laughed. 'Are you kidding? No one's read to me since I was a kid.'

'I'm serious,' Emma said. 'What do you say?'

'Oh go on then, why not?'

Emma knew the novel well and figured that Jenny would be hooked by the fourth page, and that was when she stopped reading.

'Go on,' Jenny urged her. 'You can't leave it there.'

Smiling, Emma handed her the book. 'If you want to find out what happens next . . . '

Jenny laughed again. 'Reading it

myself won't be the same. You have a very soothing voice. I'm sorry, I didn't catch your name.'

'It's Emma.' She smiled.

'Emma,' Jenny repeated. 'Well, thank you, Emma. I suppose I'm being selfish wanting you to stay, but you're the first person who hasn't stood there telling me how I'm in the best place and how everything's going to be all right and I'm in the best hands.'

'Well all of that is true.' Emma smiled again. 'But I expect you've heard it so many times it's starting to sound like a bunch of platitudes. Read the rest of the book, Jenny. You'll enjoy it.'

★ ★ ★

It was a quiet morning. Nick used it to catch up with some paperwork — hell, who was he kidding? He spent almost the entire morning trying to figure out what had been going on in Emma's life these past five years.

Checking her file, he found there was

a period of time when she hadn't worked. What was she doing then? Travelling? And then when she did return, it was part-time, so what was that all about? There was only one explanation, and that was that she must have been in a relationship, wanting to spend as much time as possible with the man in her life.

Now she was back in Yorkshire, back to full-time hours, which meant that the relationship must have failed. He was being quite the detective here, but it didn't give him any satisfaction. He felt more like a spy. Why not just ask her what she'd been doing?

Because you have no right, that's why!

A knock on his door made him jump guiltily and he called, 'Come in.'

It was Emma. Somehow he'd known it would be.

'Are you busy?'

That soft voice, that smile. Why the hell had he ever let her go? What kind of arrogance had he possessed, that he thought for one minute she would just drop everything and embark on a life abroad with him without even discussing it with her first? A very fleeting kind of arrogance, because it hadn't taken him long to realise the mistake he'd made.

'No,' he said at last. 'Come in.'

'I was just going for my break,' she said, and she seemed nervous. 'You said you'd show me the café.'

'Did I?'

'Doesn't matter. I can see you're busy.' She turned to go, but he wasn't going to let her slip away from him again. Not before he'd had the chance to put things right. He'd made her hate him, whatever she might say to the contrary, and he wanted more than anything to change that. But first he wanted to know how she felt about him now.

'I'm not busy,' he said, closing the folder on his desk and indicating the tidiness of it. 'This is a perfect time for me.' He stood and hurried over to the door, holding it open for her. 'Shall we?'

He rested his hand on her back as she passed through the door and could feel the heat of her skin through the fabric of her uniform. He withdrew his hand. That was the second time he'd touched her and felt burnt by it. Yet when she'd rested her hand on his arm earlier, she hadn't reacted in the same way.

Now they were both over the initial shock of meeting again, they were treading on eggshells. They'd had time to think things over and neither wanted to say or do the wrong thing.

'So what do you think of the Bob?' Nick asked as they walked along. *Keep it casual*, he told himself. *Keep it light*.

'Very nice,' Emma said. 'Very modern.'

'But not a lot of soul, right?' Nick laughed and her smile told him he was right. 'It'll get a personality of its own eventually.'

He pushed a glass door open into the café, and on this warm late summer day the big glass doors were propped open onto a sun-drenched patio. They were greeted by a hum of voices and the smell of fresh coffee.

'Now this,' Emma said appreciatively, 'is very nice.'

'A vast improvement on the canteen at the last place we worked together,' Nick agreed. 'Tables crammed in so you couldn't move your chair without bumping into someone, and those awful chipped tables.'

Emma laughed. 'It was pretty dreadful, wasn't it? Is that why you came here — for the trendy café?'

'Absolutely,' he said with a grin. 'Cappuccino? Do you want anything to eat? I can't say the food is much of an improvement over the old place, but it isn't bad.'

'Just the coffee, please,' she said, and he was glad because he wouldn't have felt right letting her eat alone, and he couldn't have eaten anything himself, not with his stomach tying itself up in knots.

She was still lovely. No, scratch that — she was lovelier. Her face was more defined, the delicate line of her jaw sharper, and her lips were fuller, which gave her a more contented look. She'd changed shape too, from being almost boyishly slim to growing a few curves. She'd grown up!

'Nick?'

'Sorry.' He shook himself.

'I said, shall we sit outside?'

He realised he hadn't heard her ask it the first time — wasn't even aware that she'd spoken to him. This had to stop, this drifting off into a dream world where she was concerned. There was no need for dreams anymore. She was here, she was real, and surely if he played his cards right she could be his again.

'Yes, why not,' he said distractedly. 'I'll get the coffees while you find us a table.'

He watched her go. Definitely more rounded. He smiled. He couldn't help it. She was a feast for the eyes — for his eyes anyway. Outside she looked around and chose a table well away from anyone else. She'd picked the very spot he would have chosen himself. It reminded him of how in tune they'd always been with each other. At least until he'd got things so badly wrong at the end.

He felt a prod in his back. 'Stop eyeing up the talent and move along,' a voice said. 'Some of us have patients to go back to. Although I can't say I blame you for looking.'

Nick laughed. No use denying what he'd been doing. Jimmy knew him too well for that. Jimmy was the clinical nurse manager of the NICU. They moved along the counter together.

'So that was the new midwife, yes?' Jimmy asked.

'Emma Finch,' Nick confirmed.

'Tasty.' Jimmy licked his lips. 'Spoken for?'

'Not yet,' Nick said sharply, and he didn't really know why he'd added the 'yet'.

'I see.' Jimmy grinned. 'So that's how

the land lies. You've already staked your claim to her no-doubt bounteous booty, claimed her territory as your own?'

This was starting to get difficult. 'I meant not as far as I know,' Nick said a touch tetchily, which was also a bit of a giveaway. The last thing he wanted was for Jimmy to start homing in on her. Jimmy was notorious for leaving a trail of broken hearts in his wake, which included two ex-wives and a string of fiancées.

'And you're hoping to find out, but nothing's happened yet. Okay, I can take a hint. I'll sit on my own and be lonely. Wouldn't want to cramp your style.'

No use telling Jimmy that it wasn't like that, because it was exactly like that. He couldn't deny wanting to be on his own with Emma or wanting to protect her from Jimmy's dubious charms. But most of all, he'd like to know what had left that haunting sadness in her eyes. He hadn't noticed it when they'd met first thing this morning — it had probably been eclipsed by shock; but it was there now. She looked like someone who had known hell, and he wasn't so vain to think it might be all down to him.

Her face didn't exactly light up when he joined her at the table, but there was a look of relief, as if he'd disturbed thoughts she wasn't happy about thinking. 'You're creating some interest,' he said as he opened two packs of sugar to sprinkle into his coffee. He turned his eyes to a table on the far side of the patio where Jimmy sat alone, watching them. When she looked over, Jimmy raised his coffee cup and smiled. Emma smiled back.

'He wanted to know if you were spoken for,' Nick said.

'What did you tell him?' Her eyes were teasing now. Did she know that he was fishing for his own benefit?

'I said that as far as I knew you weren't.'

'Oh.' She smiled and stirred her coffee. She wasn't going to enlighten him, and after a moment of being deep in thought she added, 'Not exactly spoken for, but I'm not free either.'

Cryptic. What did that mean? Was Rose ill? Was that why she'd come back, to take care of her aunt? He hoped that wasn't the case.

'I was looking at your employment record,' he said, then gave himself a mental kick because she looked up at him, alarm in her eyes. *Why so sad, Emma? And what are you afraid of?* That was what he really wanted to ask.

'There are no personal details on there,' he added quickly. 'Just a list of your appointments. I noticed that until you came here, you'd been working part-time.'

'I had personal reasons for that, Nick,' she said, lowering her eyes and hiding her gaze behind her long, spiky lashes. 'Do you have a problem with that?'

'Not at all,' he said and tapped his fingers on the table. This wasn't going to be at all easy, this catching-up business. He didn't want to turn it into a cold-blooded question-and-answer session.

'So what about you?' she said. 'Why did you come back, and where did your travels take you?' Her interest sounded genuine and the question was asked without bitterness.

Well, I travelled the length and breadth of this country looking for you, that's where I travelled, because as soon as you'd gone I realised what a mistake I'd made, he thought. Mistake! That was such a weak and ineffective word to describe the absolutely awful mess that was his life after she'd left — after he'd scared her away, he amended.

'I didn't go far,' he said. 'Look, shall I call Jimmy over to join us? He's going to put his neck out if he keeps craning it like that, and you should meet him anyway. He's clinical nurse manager of NICU.'

'I'd like that,' Emma said, and Nick couldn't help but think she looked relieved. 'Call him over.'

As soon as Nick beckoned to him, Jimmy was up on his feet and almost tripping over the legs of his chair in his rush to join them. Nick glanced at Emma. She was laughing, her eyes were sparkling and he realised that she might not be immune to the charms of this extremely attractive guy. He was damn good at his job, and good-looking in a tanned, fair-headed athletic kind of way.

Nick planned to make the introductions, then remember something pressing he had to attend to. He just couldn't sit here making small talk any longer, and at least this way he wouldn't be abandoning Emma altogether. But something about the way Jimmy shook her hand and held it a little too long, and the way she seemed so instantly at ease, made him remain in his seat.

Leave these two alone? God knew what might happen.

★ ★ ★

Emma sat in the big winged armchair in front of the unlit fire which would be so cosy in winter, with Keira curled up on her lap, head resting against her shoulder. She closed the book she'd been reading and kissed the top of Keira's head.

There should have been two warm little bodies sitting on her lap, one on each side. Keira and Daisy. Before they were born, Emma had decided never to dress them alike or even to give them the same initial for their first names. She hadn't tempted fate by buying the twin buggy she'd wanted, but had secretly earmarked one she'd liked.

'Have you gone to sleep?' Emma whispered.

Keira snuggled up even more. 'No, Mummy,' she said contentedly. 'I'm enjoying my cuddle.'

'So am I, darling,' Emma said. 'Very, very much.'

'Did you deliver any babies today, Mummy?' Keira asked.

'No,' Emma replied. 'It was a very

quiet day today, which was very nice for me as it was my first day. It gave me a chance to meet everyone and find my way around. There were two babies born in the unit today, but they were delivered by the other midwife on duty and they were both little boys.'

'Well, I expect you will be busier tomorrow,' Keira said in that oddly reassuring grown-up way she had.

The big event of the day had been coffee with Nick. She'd felt almost rescued by Jimmy and smiled at the thought of him. An all-round nice guy. But he wasn't Nick. And just when was she going to stop comparing all men to him? she wondered. Because if her romance with Nick were to be rekindled, always supposing he would want to start igniting flames, he would have to find out about Keira.

He'd never forgive her for not finding some way to get in touch with him. She could have contacted his father, but she hadn't. There are only so many knock-backs a girl can take. Keira looked up at her with smoky grey eyes which were identical to Nick's, and Emma knew that if Nick ever set eyes on their daughter, he would know instantly that she belonged to him. She also knew that at some point, she would have to tell him the truth. Keira was not a secret she could keep.

Later, when Keira was asleep, Emma heard a soft tap on the back door. It was Rose.

'Is she asleep?'

'Yes. I was just about to make coffee; would you like one?'

'Love one,' Rose said, and while Emma set up the coffee maker, Rose sat down at the kitchen table and sighed.

'Something wrong?' Emma asked.

'I've been worried about you,' Rose said, biting her lip. 'You were so upset this morning after that dreadful nightmare. How did it go today, really? You seemed rather quiet when you came home.'

Emma took a deep breath. Would it worry Rose even more to know what had happened at the hospital today?

She decided it would be better to be honest with her. They'd never had secrets and she didn't want to start now.

'Two quite extraordinary things happened, actually,' Emma said. 'We've got a patient expecting monoamniotic twins.'

'Like you! But it's rare, isn't it?'

'Very.'

'That must be difficult for you, Emma,' Rose said thoughtfully. 'Perhaps if you explained to someone you wouldn't have to work on that particular case.'

'I can't tell anyone, Aunt Rose,' Emma said. 'It's something I've thought long and hard about, and for the time being I don't want anyone to know anything about my private life. Which brings me to the second surprise of the day. Nick Logan.'

The colour drained from Rose's face and she put her hands flat on the table in front of her. 'Nick?' Her voice was barely a gasp. 'What's he doing there?'

'He's in charge,' Emma said with a rueful smile. She poured the coffee and placed a cup in front of Rose, then sat down opposite her. 'Are you all right?' It seemed strange to be asking Rose that question, but she looked so very shocked.

'Me?' Rose whispered. 'Fine. I'm fine. But what about you? What did he say to you? Did he . . . ? Oh, lord, Emma, perhaps you should look for a position elsewhere. I don't think you should work with Nick after what happened before.'

'That's how I felt at first,' Emma said, cupping her hands around her mug and staring thoughtfully into the steam. 'But he's been really nice.'

'Nice?' Rose hissed. 'Nice? Have you forgotten what he did?'

'No, of course not,' Emma said, bewildered by her aunt's rather vehement reaction to the mention of Nick's name. 'But I think we've all moved on since then, don't you?'

'Oh, Emma,' Rose said, reaching out and grasping her hand. 'You wouldn't take up with him again, would you?'

'No,' Emma answered quickly — she hoped not too quickly, but her answer seemed to bring immediate relief to Rose's troubled face. Now why on earth should that be?

* * *

Nick often called in on his father on his way home from the hospital, but tonight he had a particular reason to visit. He wanted to tell John exactly who the new midwife was.

Since the weather was fine, Nick went straight round to the back of the house, knowing he'd find his father working in the garden. He could see him way off in the distance down at the far end, where he had his vegetable garden and fruit trees.

'Nick!' He lifted his hand in a wave, and as always he was delighted to see him. 'Come and see this.'

Nick hurried down the gravel path through the boundary hedge between the flower garden and the vegetable patch, and joined his father by one of the three greenhouses. He certainly hadn't let being semi-retired slow him down; in fact he seemed busier now than he had when he'd worked full-time.

'What is it, Dad?'

'Hedgehog.' John Logan grinned. 'Friendly little fellow, too.'

Nick laughed and shook his head. 'Been busy, Dad?'

Nick looked around at the garden, which had been tended to within an inch of its life, then back at his father. His face was beaded with sweat and his hands were shaking. He was leaning rather heavily on a water butt and Nick wondered if he'd really wanted to show off the hedgehog, or if he felt too ill to walk up to the house and didn't want to admit it.

'You all right?'

'I think I overdid it,' John said. 'My back aches and I came over a bit dizzy.'

'When did you last have your blood pressure checked?' Nick asked, frowning.

'Oh, you know.' John waved his hand. 'It's not blood pressure. It's a bit of dehydration. I've been getting hot working out here and not drinking enough. You know how it is.'

'In that case it's time you called it a day. Come on inside, and I'll get you a drink and you can sit and sip it while I rustle us up something to eat.'

For a moment Nick thought John would turn him down, tell him not to make a fuss, but instead he bit his lip and then nodded. His quiet agreement worried Nick more than anything. He was acting like a frail old man, which was something he most certainly was not.

'I've got some news for you, Dad,' Nick said as they walked up to the house, talking partly to cover up the fact that they were walking so slowly. 'The new midwife started today. It's someone you and I both know.'

'Oh?' John stopped and looked at him. 'Does she have a name?'

'Emma Finch, but we knew her as Emma Tyler.'

'Emma,' John said. His face broke into a smile and then fell briefly. 'Finch. So she's married?'

'No, just changed her name for personal reasons.'

'Must have been a shock for both of you,' John said, starting to walk again. He was already looking better. His face had lost that grey, greasy look that had so alarmed Nick a few minutes ago. 'Mind you, it would have been more of a shock if you'd been at the interview and you'd had to face each other under those circumstances. How is she?'

'She's good,' Nick said.

'Has she forgiven you?'

Nick hesitated. There had been no question of his father taking his side when he and Emma had split up. He'd placed the blame squarely on his son's shoulders and nothing had happened since to change his mind.

'I doubt it.' Nick pushed open the kitchen door, then helped his father off with his gardening boots. 'But she seems friendly enough.'

'It would be very vain of you to believe she feels anything at all for you after all this time,' John said, his eyes narrowing as he regarded his son. 'You hurt her badly, Nick. What on earth made you do it?'

'You asked me that at the time,' Nick reminded him as he pulled a bottle of chilled water from the fridge and poured them each a glass. 'As I saw it I had two choices. I had the opportunity to go to Australia and qualify as a maternal-fetal medicine specialist, or I could stay here as an OB and hope a similar opportunity arose in this country.'

'Ironic, isn't it, that you're the best perinatologist in the area? You didn't have to go to Australia for that.'

'Dad, don't . . . ' Nick began.

'Don't what? Don't rub it in what a fool you were? I won't. I saw how you were after she left and I knew you'd made a mistake even before you did. How could you have made a huge decision like that without even talking to the girl about it? She must have felt so . . . I don't know, rejected.'

Nick had heard all this before — several times, but it still stung. 'I didn't reject her!'

'You accepted a job abroad without finding out how Emma felt about it. How did you expect her to feel? Did you seriously think she'd just drop her life here and follow you?'

That was exactly what Nick had thought, and his father could see it in his eyes. John shook his head.

'You didn't say anything before I did it, Dad.'

'Would you have listened? You were a different person then, Nick.' John's voice softened to take the edge off his words. 'A little arrogant, but understandable given how fast your career was moving and how much you were in demand.'

'I was a big-headed idiot,' Nick burst out. 'And don't I know it!'

'But you're not now,' John said calmly. 'Emma will see that. She might even fall in love with you all over again. This might be that second chance you've always wished for.'

Nick didn't reply. It was what he hoped for with all his heart, but he was afraid he was hoping for far too much.

'You do want a second chance, don't you, Nick?'

He knows me so well, he thought. When he saw her standing at the reception desk this morning it was as if someone had poured accelerant onto the flame of a candle and turned it into an inferno. He wanted her, and that was all there was to it — and it was gnawing at him like a rampant, insatiable hunger.

'You do,' John said when Nick failed to answer, and he was clearly far from displeased.

'Keep it between you and me, Dad,' Nick said. 'We only met up again today. There's a long way to go yet.'

'I won't say a word,' John said with a smile.

4

Long after going to bed, Emma was still wide awake. Seeing Nick again had brought back so many memories. Not only that, but there was also Jenny and her predicament, so like Emma's own had been. Lost in thought, she barely heard the creak of a floorboard out on the landing or saw the little shadowy figure approaching the bed.

'Are you awake, Mummy?'

'Keira! What are you doing out of bed?'

'I was too excited to sleep,' Keira said as Emma shifted over and made room for her under the duvet.

'You're freezing,' Emma said as she snuggled up. 'How long have you been up?'

'I've been sitting on my window seat looking at the stars,' Keira said, 'making wishes.'

'What did you wish for, or is it a secret?'

Keira giggled. 'I mustn't tell you,' she said, 'or it won't come true.'

'Then what are you excited about?'

Keira squeezed up her shoulders and despite the darkness, Emma knew there'd be an impish smile on her face. 'School, of course,' she said. 'I love it, Mummy.'

'Then you'd better go to sleep now,' Emma laughed, 'or you'll be falling asleep at school and missing all the fun.'

She pulled the covers up to their chins and long after Keira's breathing slowed and softened, Emma lay awake, thoughts of Nick Logan swirling about in her head.

* * *

The following morning when Emma arrived at the hospital, Nick was standing at the reception desk. He was looking over some notes and was unaware at first of her approach. His dark hair flopped forward and she could see the black sweep of his eyelashes as he flicked through the pages.

The memory of waking up next to him and admiring those lashes came back with all the force of a pile driver. The memory knocked her breath away. He'd opened his eyes, looked up at her and smiled.

'What are you thinking?' he'd asked, his voice soft and husky from sleep.

'Just how much I love you,' she'd replied tremulously, because her love for him had been so overwhelming, so all-consuming that it sometimes felt unreal.

'And I love you,' he'd replied, pulling her down to kiss him, winding his fingers in her hair, making her heart leap behind her ribs.

Two days later, he told her he was going to Australia. Had he lied about loving her? The only thing she knew for sure was that she had loved him, heart and soul.

Nick looked up suddenly, his eyebrows knitting for a moment before his expression relaxed into something more neutral. 'Ah, just the person,' he said, smiling. 'I'll need your help in about an hour.' He glanced back at the notes, then at her again. 'Are you all right?'

'Yes, fine.'

'Good.' He smiled again.

Seeing him again had brought it home to her exactly what she'd lost; what Keira had lost. He would have been a wonderful father.

'I've got Carol Masters coming in.'

'The breech baby?'

He looked up. 'You've been doing your homework,' he said, and since he was doing nothing to hide his admiration she felt ridiculously pleased. But as her first day had been relatively quiet, she'd used the time to read through the notes of some of their more problematic expectant mothers.

They'd explained to her at the interview that they took on more than the usual share of difficult pregnancies largely because they had an excellent maternal-fetal medicine specialist heading the team. She'd had no idea they were referring to Nick; she'd expected a much older man. Nick was still young for such a high position. Yet he didn't seem at all conceited. The Nick she'd known five years ago had not been one for hiding his light under a bushel, being ambitious and at times a little brash, but back then she'd thought he had every right to be. She'd been different in those days too.

'Are we going to try and turn the baby?' she asked.

'We are,' he said. 'I hope you're feeling strong.'

After a sleepless night thinking about him, she was feeling as washed-out as an old flannel, but she knew from past experience that she'd call upon that extra reserve of strength she could always rely on. Emotionally, she felt as if she'd been through a wringer, but all the same she knew she wouldn't lack the physical strength she'd need.

He made to walk away, then changed his mind. 'June tells me you've stated a preference not to work extra hours,' he said casually. 'No weekends if at all possible. Any particular reason for that?'

Yes, I like to be at home with our daughter, she thought. *My aunt has other commitments at the weekend.* But she found herself murmuring evasively, 'Rose . . . '

'Your aunt?' Once again those eyebrows were knitting in a frown. 'Is that why you came back?'

'Um, yes, I suppose. I really must go.' Emma made a vague hand signal towards the ward. 'The babies.'

'Emma,' he said quickly, 'there's no problem with you not working weekends. Really. Don't worry about it.'

She bustled away, aware of him watching her until she entered the ward. Her eyes swept over the babies sleeping at the ends of their mothers' beds. Anyone who said all babies looked the same needed their head examined. There were babies here with thick black hair, others with wisps of fine red, and some with none at all.

Some had round chubby faces, others little pointed impish faces. She walked along checking each one and chatting to the mums.

* * *

Nick remembered Rose very well and with some affection. She was the kind of woman who should have married and had a dozen children. She had the sort of home that was always warm, always welcoming.

Even on the day Nick had turned up on her doorstep in a howling gale, face like thunder, she'd invited him in. Not that he'd waited too long to be asked. He winced now when he recalled his rudeness as he pushed his way into her cosy sitting room. It was so deeply etched in his brain that he could remember what had happened almost word for word.

'Where is she?' He'd rounded on her once he was standing in the centre of the small room. 'I've just been to her flat only to be told she's gone. Gone where? Is she here?'

'She was here, Nick,' Rose had said gently. 'But she left last night.'

'What do you mean she left?' Nick had said angrily. 'Left to go where? How can she just vanish?'

'What do you expect of her, Nick?' Rose asked. 'Sit down. I'll make some coffee, but don't ask me to tell you where she is because I can't tell you.'

His anger had evaporated in the face of her kindness and he'd slumped into an armchair. He'd felt numb. 'We argued,' he said brokenly. 'Did she tell you?'

'She told me that you have accepted a new job in Australia and that your decision had ended your relationship.'

'My God,' he'd whispered. 'The fact is, Rose, I don't want to go to Australia without her. I want her to come with me. I tried to explain all this to her, but she was as mad as hell. Have you any way of contacting her?'

Rose had bitten so hard on her lip

she'd turned it white. 'I'm afraid not,' she'd said at last. 'I'm so sorry.'

'It's such a fantastic opportunity,' he went on eagerly. 'Not just for me; for both of us.'

'She thought you'd gone behind her back because you wanted an escape from your relationship,' Rose had explained.

'I know. I realise that now. It's the last thing I want. Look, Rose, she's bound to get in touch with you sooner or later. Will you tell her I have to talk to her?'

'She won't be in touch with me, Nick,' Rose had told him.

He refused to believe it. Rose was all the family Emma had.

'She won't,' she said firmly. 'Please don't come here again because I can't tell you anything.'

In the end he'd settled for her promise that she would tell Emma that he was looking for her.

'I won't give up until I find her,' he'd vowed, but wasn't that exactly what he had done? She'd left no trace behind. He'd cancelled his plans to go to Australia and instead had travelled the length and breadth of England searching for her. Every once in a while he'd knock on Rose's door asking for news, despite her asking him not to, until the day she told him that Emma had made a new life for herself and if he cared anything for her at all, he'd let her go and stop trying to hunt her down. And so the searching had stopped and he'd immersed himself in his work. But he'd never stopped hoping.

He thought again of Rose, and hoped it wasn't her ill health that had brought Emma back, but was afraid it was the most likely reason.

* * *

'I don't want to have a C-section,' Carol said firmly. 'I've talked it over with Nick and I want you to try and turn the baby round.'

Emma smiled. 'We'll do our best.

Did Nick talk to you about the possibility of complications?'

Carol nodded. 'He said there could be a cord accident or the placenta could tear and that would mean a big bleed, but that it was highly unlikely. He also said it wouldn't be painful, but . . . '

'He's a man?' Emma laughed.

'Exactly.' Carol grinned. 'I can't imagine that having my stomach pummelled and pushed is going to be entirely painless.'

'We'll do our best to make it as painless as possible,' Emma assured her. 'But I can't guarantee you won't feel some discomfort. It's a very physical procedure. And there's no guarantee that the baby won't flip round again before your due date. I see from your notes that you've been doing some exercises to try and encourage the baby to turn.'

'Yes.' Carol smiled ruefully. 'Fat lot of good it did. I'm sure this baby must be a boy. A girl would never be so stubborn.'

'Well, if you can keep doing the

exercises after this, the baby may well stay the right way round. I'm going to do an ultrasound scan before we start to check the position of the placenta, then as soon as Nick arrives, we'll get on with it.'

She didn't have to wait long. She'd barely finished smearing gel on Carol's bump when Nick walked in. He smiled at Emma, then turned the smile to Carol. Emma had almost forgotten that smile; how wonderful it felt to be on the receiving end of it.

'How are we doing?' he asked.

'We're doing just fine, thank you,' Carol replied, a slight flush filling her cheeks. It was that smile of his that had done that, Emma thought.

'Good,' he said and he turned back to Emma. 'Well, if we're all ready, we may as well get started.'

For the next ten minutes Emma and Nick pushed the baby from either side, trying to get him to turn, but stubbornly he remained in the same position. Carol's bump was blotched with red. A tear trickled down her cheek and she bit hard on her lip.

'We can stop this now,' Emma said, concerned that this was all getting too much for Carol. 'Just a word from you, Carol. We don't have to continue with this.'

'No, keep going,' Carol said. 'I want to have this baby naturally.' She looked down at her bump and added in a shaky voice. 'Turn baby, turn! Do as your mother tells you, but please do it quickly.'

Emma and Nick exchanged looks. Neither of them wanted to hurt Carol but it was clear that she was in a lot of discomfort and couldn't take much more.

'One more try and then we call it a day,' Nick said, making the decision for her. 'Ready?'

Emma nodded and Carol said, 'Go for it.'

It always looked so painful, Emma thought as she dug into the bump, but Carol was bearing it all remarkably stoically.

'Here we go,' Nick said suddenly, his

voice triumphant. 'Feel that? Emma? We have lift off! Good baby.'

Emma did indeed feel it and moments later the scan confirmed that the baby had turned.

'You did it!' Carol cried. 'Oh, thank you.' She began to cry and while Nick handed her some tissues and gave her a congratulatory hug, Emma gently cleaned the gel from her skin.

'Let's hope he stays that way,' Nick said with a grin.

'He better had,' Carol sniffed. 'I don't want to go through all that again.'

'I should go,' Nick said suddenly, noticing the time. 'Great as it's been practising my bread-making skills, I should have been at my clinic ten minutes ago. See you again soon, Carol.'

'Well, I'm not sure I appreciate my bump being likened to a lump of dough,' Carol giggled.

Emma helped her get dressed after Nick had gone.

'I'm so lucky to have him looking after me,' Carol said cheerfully. 'He must be lovely to work with.'

'Well I only started here yesterday,' Emma said with a smile. 'But no complaints so far.'

'My GP says I couldn't be in safer hands.'

'I couldn't agree more,' Emma said with a smile. 'Really. Nick's the best.'

★　★　★

Nick hurried along to his surgery, which was in the out-patients section of the hospital, pleased to have successfully turned Carol's baby. It didn't always work, but when it did, the result was often quite spectacular.

Although Emma's strength had surprised him, he was not surprised at how the effort brought a flush to her face and made a faint line of freckles stand out across her cheeks. His step lengthened as he tried unsuccessfully to walk away from his memories. It had been difficult enough to put her out of his mind when she'd been out of his life, but now she was back it was proving impossible.

He turned into the corridor leading to the consulting room. His first patient was waiting for him, the usual anxious expression on her pretty face. After three miscarriages she was pregnant again, and this time Nick was determined that she'd hang on to the baby to full term.

'Come in,' he said with a smile, holding the door open for her. 'Good to see you looking so well, Sophie.'

And he put Emma into a box at the back of his mind and closed the lid down firmly. He wouldn't have to see her again until later today, when they scanned Jenny to check everything was still okay. Until then, he intended to keep his mind on his job.

* * *

Emma waited as long as she could, but Jenny was becoming more and more restless as the time passed. 'Shall we just go ahead without Nick?' she asked at last. 'He's obviously been delayed somewhere.'

Nick had asked to be present at all Jenny's scans, but Emma didn't want to prolong the agony for the woman any longer than necessary. But there was a silly suspicious niggle at the back of her mind. This was almost a replay of what had happened to her — the midwife had gone ahead with the scan when the consultant had been delayed. She dreaded a repeat of this, and the coincidences had already been coming at her hard and fast this week, as if fate was determined to keep playing painful tricks.

'Okay,' Jenny said. 'Let's get this over with. He won't mind?'

'Not at all.'

Jenny bit down hard on her lip, obviously anticipating bad news. Emma knew how that felt. At every scan with her own pregnancy she'd been tense and worried until finally there was cause for concern, and instead of being frightened she'd become almost unnaturally calm.

'Relax,' Emma said as she looked up at the screen and smiled. 'It's all looking good so far.'

It did, too. Both babies were thriving. Emma breathed a huge sigh of relief and gave Jenny a dazzling smile. 'The scan shows both babies are still doing fine.'

'But that could change at any time,' Jenny said anxiously. 'They said there was some tangling of the cords at my last scan.'

'The cords have probably been tangled since your first trimester,' Emma explained. 'The babies will have had more room to move about then and some tangling is almost inevitable. But that doesn't have to be serious. Even lone babies have been known to get themselves tied up in knots. It's only if one of the cords becomes compressed that we would be concerned.'

'That would be dangerous?'

'Yes,' Emma said. 'That's why we'll deliver by C-section no later than 36 weeks.'

'I don't think that any of you people really understand how frightened I am,'

Jenny burst out. 'You keep coming out with all this reassurance, but I wouldn't be here if my babies weren't in danger, would I?'

'No, you wouldn't,' Emma said. 'But as you're here, you should be making the most of all this bed rest. Once those babies are born you won't have a minute to yourself, and with two of them to look after you'll be wishing for time to put your feet up.'

Despite her anxiety, Jenny smiled up at Emma. 'You really think they have a chance?'

'Of course I do,' Emma said reassuringly.

The door opened and Nick rushed in. 'I'm so sorry,' he said. 'My clinic took longer than I expected today. How are things?'

'Fine,' Emma said. 'Everything is as it should be.'

He came over and checked the screen and his smile said it all. 'Everything still looking as it should,' he said. 'Well done, Jenny. That's another day closer to a safe delivery. How are you feeling?'

'Actually,' Jenny said, 'since Emma's been talking to me, I've felt a little better about all this.'

'Good, that's great news, Jenny,' Nick said with a grin. Then he turned to Emma. 'When you've finished in here, Emma, could I have a word in my office, please?'

'Sure,' she said, nodding. What would he want to talk to her about? A patient? Or did he feel this uneasy professional relationship wasn't really working out? Was he going to ask her to leave?

'Are you all right, Emma?' Jenny asked, frowning.

'Me? I'm fine,' Emma said and decided to be honest. 'Just wondering what the boss wants to see me about.'

As it happened, as soon as Emma left Jenny she was called into one of the labour rooms. A nice straightforward second baby was on its way and doing everything by the book. This was the part of her job that Emma loved best. She enjoyed looking after the expectant mothers, and after the birth she loved to handle the babies and help the new mums put them to the breast for the first time. The moment of birth when pain suddenly turned to joy, and tears of happiness flowed, was the most rewarding part of all.

And this birth was truly textbook. Emma had admitted the mother just four hours ago and the labour had been progressing steadily ever since. Alison had required no pain relief and there was no tear in spite of the speed of the rapid second stage. Emma wrapped the baby girl in a green cloth and passed her straight to her mother.

'Say hello to your daughter,' she said. 'Congratulations both of you. She's beautiful.'

The father gazed at his wife and baby with a mixture of adoration and wonder on his face. He'd completely forgotten about the camera he'd brought in with him, but there would be time for photographs in a while when the placenta had been delivered and Alison had been made comfortable.

'Why isn't she crying?' Alison asked, looking concerned. 'I thought all newborn babies bawled their heads off.'

'Not necessarily.' Emma smiled. 'And in a few days' time you'll be asking why she never stops crying! Look at her. She's busy giving you the once-over, seeing what the parents she's been listening to these past few months actually look like.'

'She is, too,' Alison whispered softly. 'Do you like what you see, darling girl?'

'Does she have a name yet?' Emma asked.

'Daisy,' Alison said and it was all Emma could do to keep the smile on her face from turning into an expression of horror.

Daisy! How many more of these reminders would she have to bear this week? Her own little Daisy should have been at school right now with Keira. She could even imagine them walking into the school side by side, hand in hand.

'What a lovely name,' she said hoarsely.

But the happy parents were far too engrossed to notice Emma's sudden distress.

It didn't get past Audrey, the healthcare assistant helping her. 'Are you all right?' she whispered. 'You've gone as white as a sheet.'

'F-fine,' Emma stammered.

'You don't want me to get anyone?'

'No, I told you, I'm fine,' Emma said, then smiled, aware that she'd spoken harshly. 'I'm sorry, I didn't mean to snap.'

She was far from fine. On a personal level this was turning into the week from hell. It was as if the past had come back to haunt and torture her with a vengeance. She turned herself on to automatic pilot and carried on with what she had to do, even managing a few cheerful quips with the new parents. By the time she'd finished in the labour room, her shift was over and it was time to leave. She did the handover, then went to fetch her coat.

Daisy. She bunched up her coat against her face. Oh, Daisy! She remembered Daisy's silence. She hadn't made a sound, not once in her short life. And she'd been identical to Keira. They would have been like two little peas in a pod. Once she had Daisy in her arms, she'd talked to her non-stop, whispering words of love, praying for a miracle; but Daisy slipped peacefully and silently away. As long as Emma lived, she would never forget that moment when she knew Daisy had gone, but she didn't let them take her away immediately. She'd held on to her, wishing there was some way to breathe life back into that tiny body.

Those last minutes would be with her forever. The despair, the anguish, the grief. She'd even cried over Keira when she'd finally got to hold her — tears of joy and sadness all mingled together. And the worst pain of all was thinking that it could so easily have been both of them that she'd lost. If she hadn't had

Keira, she would have had nothing. The thought of how close Emma had come to losing Keira brought fresh tears she just couldn't hold back.

She muffled her sobs in her coat. She hadn't cried like this for Daisy for a long time except in waking from nightmares, and now she'd started, she didn't think she'd ever stop because this waking grief was so much more intense than the sleeping kind. It was true what they said — you never got over losing someone precious; you just learned to live with it, and sometimes grief could rear up and overwhelm you when you least expected it. She didn't hear the door open and close; hadn't expected anyone to come into the room now that the shift change was over. In fact, she wasn't aware of the presence of anyone else until she felt a hand on her shoulder. She jerked away, pulled the coat from her face and saw Nick, a look of confusion on his face. Confusion and pain.

'Emma! Whatever is the matter?'

Seeing him made her feel even worse. He should have been there for the birth of his babies. He should have had the chance to say goodbye to Daisy. She began to cry even harder.

'Emma?'

He gave her a helpless look, then pulled her against him. The feel of his chest against her cheek, and the warmth of him, were all too familiar, all too wonderful. Too late, she remembered she was supposed to be meeting him in his office.

'I'm sorry,' she murmured.

'What for? Standing me up or making my shirt all wet?'

She backed away a little and looked up at him. Oh, how she'd longed for this, to feel the comfort of his arms around her, to hear the beat of his heart against her face again.

'For this,' she said. 'The tears. I don't know what came over me.'

'Well, I've seen some people get a bit emotional after a delivery, but nothing on this scale,' he said, still looking bemused. 'Or is there something more to these tears?' He tilted her chin, then pulled a tissue from the box on the windowsill and began to mop her face, one hand under her chin, the other gently dabbing. 'There, that's better,' he said, and the sudden gentleness in his tone almost tore her heart out.

She tried to smile, to convince him that all was well, but her lips wobbled alarmingly. How different the birth of their twins would have been if he'd been there.

'You're not all right at all, are you?' he said, his brow creasing. 'Is it your aunt?'

'Oh, no, nothing like that,' Emma said, shaking her head. 'It's just . . . ' She fumbled around trying to find a believable reason for her tears, and decided on the truth, or at least part of it. 'The baby I delivered — they called her Daisy. It just reminded me of another Daisy. I lost her. She . . . she died.'

He sat down on the edge of the table

and took hold of both her hands in his, looking deep into her eyes. 'You never forget those lost babies, do you?' he said, his voice heavy with sadness. 'And sometimes all it takes is a name to bring it all back. Well, it's clear you're in no state to drive just yet, Emma. Will you join me for a coffee before you go?'

'Oh, I should be going really.' Emma thought of Keira. She'd be waiting at Aunt Rose's, eager to tell her about her day, and she was already late. 'I have to be getting along. Aunt Rose will be expecting me.'

'Then leave your car here and let me drive you home,' he said.

'To Wiltonthorpe? But it's such a long way, and . . . no, I can't let you do that.'

'What if I insist?'

Amazing how fear knocked aside everything else. She tore her hands out of his and struggled to get into her coat. 'It really isn't necessary, Nick,' she said as she fought to get her arm in the sleeve. Nick grabbed the coat and held it for her, his hands lightly touching her neck as he turned her collar down.

'When your hair was long, it used to get caught inside your coat, do you remember?' he asked raggedly as if he, too was tortured by memories. But that couldn't be. He was the one who'd pushed her out of his life, not the other way around.

She remembered her long hair. He used to help her with her coat and then he'd pull her hair out, and his fingers would always linger, and he'd say how soft her hair was and how much he loved touching it.

'It suits you short,' he went on. 'It shows off your neck. You have a lovely neck, Emma.'

She had her back to him. Was that a catch in his voice? She felt his fingers on her neck, stroking her skin, and shivers trickled down her spine. His touch was so familiar, so missed. She willed her body to stiffen, to show that she didn't appreciate this intimacy, but instead her spine turned to rubber and she leaned back against him.

And then he was kissing her neck, sliding his arms around her. She ached for his touch and it was as if they'd never broken up. As if he hadn't broken her heart and left her.

She turned around so that his hands were on her back and looked into his beautiful eyes that were dark with desire. He looked as lost as she felt.

His lips took an age to reach hers and when they did, the effect was explosive, blowing apart her resolve, knocking her legs from under her and making her respond with a passion she'd forgotten she possessed.

Even as she revelled in his kiss, she knew she had to stop this and pulled away. 'Nick, I . . . '

'No,' he said, shaking his head as if emerging from a trance. 'I shouldn't have. I'm so sorry, Emma. You just seemed so upset, and I only meant to comfort you. I should never have let things get so out of hand. Please forgive me.'

'I should go,' she said unevenly. 'K
. . . Rose will be waiting.'

'Of course,' he said, but he looked
more worried than ever. 'Well, if you're
sure you're all right to drive. I'd hate to
let you leave here and then you have an
accident.'

'What was it that you wanted to see
me about?' she asked as gradually her
heart rate began to return to normal
and the heat faded slowly from her cheeks.

'Nothing urgent. Tomorrow will do,'
he said, but he was still looking at her.
'Are you absolutely certain there's
nothing else wrong?'

'I'm fine.' She rubbed her tears away
with a brisk sweep of the back of her
hand. 'Fine, really.'

'No you're not,' he said. 'And I
haven't made things any easier for you.
I'm sorry, Emma, I won't let anything
like that happen again.'

He turned and walked out of the
room. Emma took some deep breaths
and tried to make sense of what had
happened.

Once safely inside his own office, Nick closed the door and leaned back against it, shutting his eyes and seeing only Emma's stricken face. She'd seemed so vulnerable, so small and so desperately in need of comfort that he couldn't resist holding her. There must have been more to it than she was admitting. And it must be Rose. There was no other explanation. Rose must be ill.

And crass, insensitive idiot that he was, he'd kissed her neck for heaven's sake. When she'd turned in his arms, how was he supposed to resist kissing her when she held her face up to his? Most shocking of all, she didn't seem to mind at all. In fact her hunger had startled him. But she was upset and he'd taken advantage, and that was unforgivable. He felt like a monster, the very worst sort of man there was. And he didn't like himself very much.

The last thing she needed was to feel under any kind of pressure from him right now. Perhaps it would be prudent to withdraw a little, pull back, put their relationship where it belonged, on a professional-only basis. Not just prudent, but downright sensible. The way she'd felt in his arms just now had been so good; had brought back so many memories. He wanted her back, but time had taught him that just wanting something didn't mean you could have it.

5

The next day triggered a busy period in the maternity wing, with mothers almost queuing up to deliver their babies and extra staff having to be called in. Little Daisy went home the day after her birth and Emma was quite relieved to see the back of her. Not that she wasn't a beautiful, adorable baby, but it meant that she wouldn't have to hear the name again.

By the weekend, Emma was ready for two days off and the chance to catch her breath and spend some time with Keira. But on Saturday morning, Keira announced that she was going to the swimming pool with Suki and her mother and having lunch in town afterwards. Emma was torn between disappointment at missing precious time with Keira and joy that her daughter had already made such a firm friend.

Suki's mother, Mai, called to collect Keira at nine o'clock. 'We won't be late back,' she promised. 'And I'll be in the pool with them at all times, so there'll be no danger. It's a special kiddies' pool.'

'It's so kind of you,' Emma said.

Mai's eyes sparkled. 'Not at all,' she said. 'It's lovely for Suki to have someone to play with. Make the most of your quiet morning.'

Emma knew she should spend the time catching up with housework and washing, but today there was something more pressing she had to do. As soon as Keira had gone, she picked some flowers from the garden and walked across the road to the little church.

The village was so quiet. She passed a man pushing his bike up the hill on his way to the little shop to buy a newspaper. He called out a cheery greeting. Then she passed a couple walking a pair of spaniels who also called out to her. This whole place felt like home, she thought as she pushed open the little wooden gate and stepped into the shady churchyard to walk along the path softened by overnight rain.

Her grandparents were buried here. In fact generations of her mother's family were here. It really added to her sense of belonging to feel that connection with the past. But it was the more recent past she wanted to connect with right now.

Daisy had been buried with Emma's grandparents in the shadow of an old oak tree. The big old stone bore her grandparents' names, but there was a small memorial vase in the centre with Daisy's name inscribed on it. Emma hadn't been able to afford a bigger memorial.

She removed the dying flowers she'd left a week ago and washed out the vase, then carefully arranged the fresh flowers in their place. 'I'm working with your daddy now, Daisy,' she murmured as she threaded the stems of flowers through the holes. 'I can't say it's easy, but we're managing. I think we might even develop a good working relationship in time.' She smiled. 'He's a very good doctor. He's so kind and thoughtful. He would have adored you and your sister. Keira isn't with me today because she's gone swimming with a new friend from school.'

Sometimes it felt silly to ramble on, telling Daisy about the events of the past week, but it made her feel closer somehow. Often she didn't cry when she visited the grave, and she was sure that her tears earlier in the week were because of the unexpected shock of hearing Daisy's name coming on top of having a patient expecting monoamniotic twins.

Everything could be explained, she thought. There was a reason for everything. She shuddered. What was Nick's reason for forcing their break-up? Had he simply fallen out of love with her? Or hadn't he been in love with her at all?

She stood up, her knees stiff. She'd been here for much longer than usual.

After a whispered goodbye, she turned to leave and walked right into a solid wall which turned out to be Nick's chest.

She gasped with shock and dropped the dying flowers on the ground. How could he be here, large as life? He was wearing jeans and a dark brown leather jacket and he looked devastatingly handsome.

'What are you doing here?' she cried furiously, wondering how long he'd been standing behind her, how much he'd heard.

'I'm sorry,' he said, sounding genuinely apologetic. 'I didn't mean to startle you. I've been over by the gate for some time, but it seemed as if you were never going to leave, so I thought I'd better come over. Are you all right?'

'Of course I'm all right,' she snapped and bent to pick up the flowers, blinded by a sudden rush of tears.

'I'll get those,' he said, sweeping them up in an instant in his capable hands.

'What are you doing here?' she

demanded, aware that he was looking past her, trying to read the words on the headstone. Would he notice the much newer vase in the centre? Would he be able to read the words which were only partially covered by the flowers?

'Your grandparents?' he asked gently. 'Harold and Madeleine Finch.'

'Please,' she said, half angrily, half despairingly. 'You shouldn't be here. This is an intrusion on my private time. What do you think you're doing here, anyway?'

'Well I came to see you and there was no one at your house, so I thought I'd take a walk round the village and I spotted you in here.' He seemed puzzled at her reaction to him being here.

He'd been to her house? She reeled with shock. What if Keira hadn't gone out with Suki? It was more than likely that she would have been the one to open the door and if she had, it would have only taken one look at those grey eyes for Nick to know the truth. And if Keira hadn't been at the house, then she would have been right here, right now.

'You had no right,' she said, walking briskly away from the grave before he could study it any more closely. 'I can just about tolerate seeing you at the hospital, but I won't have you pushing your way in to my private life, do you understand?'

He followed her, paused to drop the flowers in the bin by the gate, then walked out into the street. 'Tolerate?' he said, blinking, confused. 'I thought we were okay, Emma. I don't understand. Why the sudden hostility?'

'What happened yesterday was a mistake,' she cried, her voice wavering.

'I know,' he said, his eyes darkening with what she hoped was regret but looked more like agony. 'We'd already established that and I've said it won't happen again. Surely you don't despise me that much?'

She stopped abruptly, gulping in

lungfuls of the clean, fresh air. 'I don't despise you,' she muttered.

'Your grandparents died before you were born,' he said, sounding more baffled than ever. 'You seem disproportionately upset over someone you never met.'

She spun round to face him and dug her hands deep into her pockets. 'Just promise me that you'll never come here again,' she said urgently.

He shrugged. 'All right, if that's what you want. I just wanted to see you away from the hospital, that's all.'

'Why?'

Why? He stared down at her. She was almost seething with anger because he was here and he couldn't give her a reason. To say he just wanted to make sense of things wasn't a reason. He was worried about her. But that wasn't much of a reason either. He'd had time to think over his decision that he'd be cool with her and knew that wasn't possible, so why was he here? The truth was, he didn't know, except he needed to see her again away from work.

She was looking up at him, waiting for an answer.

'Do I take it you're not going to ask me in for coffee then?' he said with a grin.

She seemed to soften a little and for a moment he thought he'd broken though, but then she threw up the barriers again.

'I'm very busy,' she said brusquely. 'I have a lot to do.'

'Does your aunt still live over there?' He nodded towards a house on the other side of the road adjoining Emma's stone cottage.

'She does.'

'Remember how we used to walk up the hill past the sheep after one of Rose's Sunday lunches?' he said, his eyes clouding like mist on the moors. 'We could see for miles from up there.'

'I really don't recall,' she said. She was lying. He knew that. And she was rattled. Was she close to admitting the truth, which was that she still had feelings for him? Was that why his presence here unsettled her so?

And if she did admit there was still something between them, could it work? Absolutely it could work. He would make it work. If she'd only give him a chance.

'I'm sorry you've had a wasted journey, Nick,' she said abruptly. 'But I really do have a mountain of things to do.' She turned to go and would have stepped into the road right in front of a car if he hadn't grabbed her and pulled her back.

The car driver leaned on his horn and shook his head, then put his foot down and sped away. Nick pulled her against him and wrapped his arms around her, devastated at how close she'd come to being knocked down and all too aware that it was his fault.

This was more than just wanting her, much more, and he knew it. Now she was back, he wasn't going to let her go. He knew he couldn't keep any promises to stay away from her.

The car had been so close that Emma had felt it touch her sleeve. If Nick hadn't been there to pull her back she'd have been hit, maybe even killed. But if Nick hadn't been there, she wouldn't have walked blindly into the road in the first place.

She wriggled out of his arms. 'Let go of me,' she said, pushing him away and registering the look of horror on his face.

'You almost got yourself killed. Stupid . . . '

'Stupid? Perhaps you shouldn't have pulled me back! Then I'd be out of your life for good, wouldn't I?'

He ran his hand through his hair and backed away from her. 'How can you say that?' he said brokenly. 'The last thing I want is you out of my life. I didn't mean you were stupid. I was talking about myself.'

He suddenly looked vulnerable. Shock had left him wide open. Was it possible his feelings for her were more than physical? She couldn't allow herself to think that. It was much too dangerous. Things hadn't worked out between them before; there was no reason to suppose they would now.

'Don't come back here again, Nick,' she said softly. 'I mean it. If you won't leave me alone I'll move, and this time it will be for good, do you understand?'

He flung up his hands in exasperation. 'No, Emma, actually I don't understand,' he choked wretchedly. 'There's still something there between us. You can't deny that. The way you kissed me yesterday was no one-off fluke.'

'*You* kissed *me!*' she reminded him as she struggled to keep control of her raging emotions.

'And you didn't object,' he reminded her, his voice now gentle. He reached out and touched the side of her face, his fingers threading through the soft, short waves of her wind-ruffled hair and despite herself, she leaned her head into his hand. His eyes looked over her face and finally came to rest on her eyes. 'We can't brush this under the carpet. We have to talk about it.'

'There's nothing to talk about,' she insisted, stepping back so that he had to drop his hand. Too dangerous to stay close. Too risky to let him anywhere near her.

'I think there is. You can't go on ignoring it, Emma. It's not going to go away, and I'm not going to go away. What we had before was . . . '

'Ended abruptly and without warning by you,' she cried as old pains were once again revived. 'I can't take that risk again, Nick.'

'That's why we have to talk,' he said. 'We have to clear up the misunderstanding that . . . '

'Misunderstanding?' It was her turn to throw up her hands in exasperation. 'Excuse me, Nick. I like working with you — heck, I even like you, though God knows why — but don't ask me to swallow rubbish about a misunderstanding. You dropped me, remember?'

'No, I don't actually,' he said, sparks

of anger beginning to flicker in his eyes. 'I'm sick of taking the blame for what happened. You were the one who ran away and ignored my pleas for you to get in touch.'

'What?'

'All my messages you ignored, refusing to tell me where you were. I must have left dozens . . . '

She continued staring at him blankly. She really didn't know what he was talking about.

'You really don't know,' he whispered hoarsely. 'You really have no idea.'

Two minutes ago, Emma wanted him gone. Now she wanted explanations. What did he mean? What pleas? She'd heard nothing. As for messages, she hadn't received any messages. Who would he have left messages for her with?

'Perhaps you'd like to tell me,' she said at last.

He looked at his watch. 'I'm sorry,' he said, infuriatingly refusing to enlarge on what he'd said. 'I should go. I've been here too long already.'

'Nick!'

But it was too late. He'd turned and was already striding back down the hill to where he'd left his car, his back so straight, his head held high. Emma watched him all the way down and saw him get into his car, a low silver sporty number, spin it round and drive out of the village. Only when he'd gone did she cross the road to her cottage.

'Emma!' Rose called to her as she was going inside. 'Was that Nick I saw you talking to?'

Emma waited for Rose to join her before going into the cottage. 'Yes, it was,' she sighed. 'Would you like a coffee?'

'What was he doing here?' Rose demanded as they entered Emma's cottage. 'Sit down, Emma, I'll make the coffee. You look as if you've had a shock. What did he say? Did he say something to upset you?'

Emma didn't feel like arguing and sank into a chair.

'I'll do instant,' Rose said. 'I don't know how to work that machine. Are you going to tell me what he was doing here? And where's Keira?'

The second question was easy to answer. The first was far more difficult because Emma didn't really know the answer herself. Nick had apparently come to tell her he still felt something for her and then when she'd started asking questions, he'd rushed to get away.

'I think he came here to tell me he still has feelings for me,' she said, and felt that even that was understating it.

Rose paled as she always seemed to when Nick was mentioned. 'Did he come into the cemetery?' Rose asked. 'Did he see? Did he say anything?'

'He didn't see anything,' Emma said, chewing the corner of her mouth thoughtfully. He hadn't seen anything but he'd been suspicious.

'Well, what are you going to do?' Rose said worriedly.

'Do? Well the only thing I can do is

face up to it,' Emma said resolutely. 'We have no problem working together. As long as we can keep our relationship strictly professional, we'll be okay, but he doesn't seem to want that.'

'And what about Keira?'

'He's not to know about Keira,' Emma said sharply. 'I know I should have told him five years ago that I was pregnant, and I tried, but he'd gone. What if he started demanding access? What if he can't forgive me?'

'That's what really worries you, isn't it?' Rose sighed. 'That he'll hate you for not telling him. But it wasn't your fault, Emma. You tried to contact him. It wasn't your fault that he'd gone away.'

'Yes, but I've kept this secret from him all these years. How do you think that will make him feel? To find out that I have deprived him of five years of his daughter's life?'

She gnawed on her lip. She couldn't bear it if he ended up hating her, and yet she felt sure that he would, in the end.

* * *

The following Monday Emma arrived at the hospital to find that Carol had been admitted the previous evening.

'Baby hasn't flipped back into the breech position,' June said cheerfully. 'And that's the good news. The bad news is that this labour isn't going anywhere. It's been stop-start with weak contractions all over the place. I've used prostaglandin gel to ripen the cervix. Hopefully that will be enough to get things started.'

Emma nodded. Only when labour was properly underway could they be assured that the baby wouldn't suddenly decide to turn.

'You can help by walking around, Carol,' Emma said. 'Some gentle exercise might encourage things to start moving. Your husband can walk with you — just up and down the corridor out here.'

'I'll be off then,' June said with a smile. 'You'll be in safe hands with Emma. And I've paged Nick. He said he wanted to be here for this one.'

'Oh,' Emma said breezily. 'Right.'

She left Carol and her husband Ian to slowly walk the corridor and went to see how Jenny was getting along. She found her still looking miserable and bored.

'Isn't there anything you could do to pass the time?' Emma said. 'Have you given up reading? How about doing a little knitting?'

'I can't concentrate to read and I don't know how to knit,' Jenny said glumly. 'I don't get on with crossword puzzles and I can't even sew a button on. I'm pretty useless.'

'I'll bring some knitting needles and wool in tomorrow,' Emma said as she plumped up Jenny's pillows. They didn't really need plumping, but she wanted Jenny to feel a little cosseted. It was all too easy to fade into the background when you were brought in for bed rest. You almost became part of the furniture. At least, that was how Emma had felt.

'It won't do any good,' Jenny sighed. 'I'm all thumbs.'

'I'll show you how to knit. You can knit some squares and we can donate them to charity. You'd be surprised how many people can make use of them.'

'Really?'

'Oh, yes,' Emma said, nodding.

Even if the squares were just sewn together and handed in to an animal home, they would be put to good use. And there was nothing like knitting for passing the time, or so Emma had found. It was also a very calming activity.

'But you won't have time to teach me,' Jenny said. 'You're always so busy.'

'I have breaks,' Emma said with a smile. 'Honestly, Jenny, when I . . . ' She broke off just in time. She'd almost admitted that she'd been in the same position as Jenny once and had found peace in knitting, and that she must not do. 'When I found myself with time on my hands,' she continued, hoping Jenny hadn't noticed her sudden stall, 'I found knitting helped a lot. And I still find that it helps me unwind.'

'Squares?' Jenny asked, eyes twinkling.

'Baby clothes,' Emma said. 'I make tiny things for the preemie babies. In actual fact, I use patterns for dolls clothes as they have to be so small. Rather fiddly, but very rewarding.'

While she chatted, Emma checked the monitor. 'So far so good,' she said, beaming. 'Looking good, Jenny.'

* * *

The first thing Nick saw when he entered the unit was Carol and her husband Ian walking the corridor. In answer to his puzzled look, Ian explained, 'Emma thought some mild exercise might hurry things along.'

'Yes, good idea,' Nick said. 'Feeling okay, Carol?'

'I just want it over with,' she said. 'I feel as if I've been pregnant forever.'

'Well, it won't be much longer now.' Nick grinned and at that moment spotted Emma coming out of the side room. His smile faded. 'Excuse me.'

He hurried forward. 'Emma, could I see you for a moment?' he called and beckoned her to his office.

She looked up and even at a distance he could see the flush in her cheeks.

He was already sitting behind his desk when she entered.

'You wanted to see me?'

'We haven't resolved anything between us,' he said and lifted his hand slightly when she opened her mouth to protest. 'Please, hear me out on this. You've only been back just over a week, but believe me, I knew the minute I saw you that as far as my feelings for you are concerned, nothing has changed.'

'Please, Nick, no, don't say that.'

'I'm aware that you are uncomfortable with that.' He hesitated.

'Not uncomfortable, Nick,' she said, helping him. 'Confused.'

'Yes, yes, I know.' He ran his hand through his hair. 'Understandable. It's all turned out to be a bit of a mess, hasn't it? I'm not going to push matters, but I just want you to know that if you change your mind about me . . . Oh, hell, Emma. You just have to say the word, you know?'

'And what word would that be?' she teased, trying to lighten the atmosphere which had become so tense she felt as if she might suffocate.

'Don't make fun of me, Emma,' he said.

It hadn't been her intention at all. She would never make fun of Nick, ever. 'I wasn't. Is that all?'

'For now,' he said, getting to his feet and hurrying to the door, intending to open it for her; but when he got there, he couldn't do it. He wanted to do the right thing, the honourable thing, whatever the hell that was, but with her so close it was impossible.

'Are you going to let me out of here, Nick?'

He looked down at her. She hadn't run anywhere, so what was making her so breathless? Him? It had to be. If so, then why was she denying her feelings for him?

The pupils of her eyes were so large that they almost obliterated the summer blue, and the flush in her cheeks intensified. With one fluid movement she was in his arms again, and he had no idea how it had happened. They were like magnets, constantly drawn together. He hated this — hated being out of control; but when she was around it seemed he had no will of his own. And this kind of behaviour wasn't him. He'd never had to use force on a woman. Not that he was using force now. She was making no effort to get away.

'What are you doing?' she said, but the indignation and anger in her words were softened by confusion.

He was so close he could smell her hair. A faintly fruity scent; delicious, like her. He closed his eyes. If he tried to kiss her again, what would she do? Hit him? He almost wished she would.

He opened his eyes and found her looking up at him. Her lips seemed to have softened and were parting almost expectantly. He moved his hand from the door and cupped the back of her head.

'Did I tell you I like your hair like this?' he said with gravel in his voice. 'Suits you.'

'Yes,' she whispered. 'You did.'

This was pure agony. He'd missed her. There had been no one like her before or since. He trailed his fingers through her silken hair, watching as it fell back into place. Was she breathing? She seemed to be holding her breath. He could kiss her right now and he sensed she wouldn't put up any kind of a fight. The temptation was huge — overpowering; but he could not, must not let this happen again. He lowered his head and she tilted hers back, lips parting more, inviting him.

Emma's heart hurtled against her ribs at a hundred miles an hour. His lips were soft yet demanding, and she couldn't even begin to stop herself clinging to him as if her life depended on it.

There was no denying this any longer. He wanted her; she wanted him. They were made for each other, destined to be together, and it was going to take some kind of catastrophe to keep them apart.

'Oh, Emma,' he murmured. 'If you knew how much I wanted you . . . '

'Nick, we can't,' she said, but she was unable to pull away.

'Can't we? Why not?' His breath was hot and sweet against her ear now.

'It's been so long,' Emma said. 'Things have changed.'

'Our feelings for each other haven't,' he said. But that wasn't what she meant. She meant that in five years so much had changed. The attraction between them hadn't, but life had.

A sharp knock on the door had them springing apart.

'What is it?' Nick rapped, turning his back to Emma and flinging open a filing cabinet drawer. Emma leaned against the wall, breathless.

Audrey opened the door and popped

her head round.

'Sorry to interrupt,' she said, looking from Nick to Emma. She would have to be blind not to see she'd walked in on something pretty big.

'What is it, Audrey?' Emma asked, her voice strained.

'Carol,' Audrey said. 'She's back in bed. Are you all right, Emma? You look terribly flushed.'

'I'm fine. I'll be right there,' Emma said coolly. 'Thank you.'

Wow, she sounded so calm! She surprised herself with just how controlled she seemed when inside all was a tumultuous mess. It was Nick who seemed the most disturbed. He still kept his back to her. What was going on with him? He never used to be like this. Back then, back when they were together, she'd teased him, calling him the ice-man because he was so cool about their relationship when they were at work. Now look at him. He was almost helpless and couldn't seem to keep his hands off her. He looked over his shoulder at her, his eyes glittering.

'If there's nothing else . . . ' Emma said, letting her words hang in the air between them. 'I mean if we're finished here, I'll go.'

He turned to face her. 'I wish to God I was finished with you, Emma,' he said huskily. 'Believe me, I don't like this any more than you do, but I don't know what the hell to do about it.'

She turned and left his office, confusion raging through her. She pushed it all away from her mind and entered the side room.

Carol was back in bed. 'I don't want to walk up and down any more,' she said. 'I'm fed up. I just want this baby to be born. Can't you do something to speed it up?'

'Let me examine you,' Emma said. 'We'll see how things are going.'

It only took a moment and the news was disappointing. Carol's cervix was only just over three centimetres dilated.

'It will be a while yet, Carol,' Emma said. 'I'm afraid you're just going to have to be patient for a bit longer. I know it's difficult, but once things start moving it will be over very quickly. I'll check again in a while and if things still aren't moving, I'll rupture the membranes.'

'Will that work?' Ian asked.

'It often does,' Emma said, nodding. 'I'll have a little listen to the baby's heart to make sure he's still happy in there.'

He was. There was no sign of distress coming from the baby. If only his mother could be as relaxed about all this as her baby!

* * *

Nick paced his office furiously like a caged beast. He wanted her. Wanted her more than he'd ever wanted anything in his life. His rekindled feelings for her were stronger than ever. But did they have a future? Could they? He only knew that he'd never wanted anything or anyone as much as he wanted her

— and it was for life, not just for a quick fling. Wonderful as that would be, he wanted more.

He opened his door and she happened to be passing. He watched the gentle sway of her hips and felt his mouth dry up. Impossible. This was just impossible. *Get a grip, you fool*, he thought despairingly. *Accept that it's over. It was over five years ago and it's no less over now.* Except the way she kissed him told him it was far from over.

'Emma,' he called her name, and she stopped and turned slowly. 'Carol?'

'No progress as yet,' she said, walking back towards him, and now there was compassion in her eyes as if she felt sorry for him. Her anger he could have dealt with — a slap around the face, even. But this? Pity? Why? Why pity him?

The doors at the end of the corridor burst open with a crash and Nick's father walked in, pushing a frail-looking girl in a wheelchair.

'What on earth?' Nick muttered as he

and Emma both ran forward as one.

'Emma,' John Logan said, the tension on his face relieved momentarily by pleasure at seeing her again. 'Great to see you. Nick, this is Melanie.'

'Who?' Nick was puzzled, sure he'd never seen this girl before.

'She's from the traveller's site. She's eighteen years old and twenty-seven weeks pregnant.'

'Dad, what is this?' Nick ground out the words. His father was supposed to be semi-retired; what on earth was he doing getting involved with the travellers? No wonder he always looked so damned tired. He'd cut his hours back at the hospital only to make them up elsewhere.

'Emma, would you take Melanie and make her comfortable, please?' John said. 'I'll be along in a moment. Melanie, Emma will take care of you now, dear, okay?'

'Thank you, Doctor Logan,' the girl said nervously. She seemed totally overawed by everything and John gave her shoulder a gentle squeeze.

'You'll be okay, Melanie,' he said, then moved to one side with Nick while Emma took the wheelchair and pushed Melanie towards an empty side room.

'I've been looking after a couple of pregnant women on the site,' he explained. 'It only costs a few minutes of my time at most every week and I can spot any potential problems before they become dangerous. Don't look at me like that, Nick. I've tried to fill my hours at home, but there's only so much gardening a man can do.'

'What is the use of you retiring at all if you're going to do things like this?' Nick began, then shook his head. 'Okay, what's Melanie's story?'

'I saw her for the first time today. She's only just told her mother that she's pregnant. Nick, she has a BP of 160 over 90 and she hasn't seen a doctor at all until she saw me.'

Nick whistled through his teeth. 'Right,' he said. 'Thanks for bringing her in, Dad. Is anyone coming in to be with her?'

'They don't trust hospitals,' John said grimly. 'I had a heck of a fight on my hands getting them to let me bring her in with me. I've got a couple of calls to make round the hospital and I'll call back later to see if there's any news for the family. Look after her, Nick.'

'I always look after my patients, Dad,' Nick replied.

'I was talking about Emma,' John said quietly and then he smiled that all-knowing smile of his. 'You mustn't let her go this time.'

'And if she wants to go, I can't stop her either,' Nick replied stiffly.

'I don't believe you'd give up that easily,' John said. 'Not a second time.'

Nick turned and followed Emma into the side room, where she had already got Melanie into a hospital gown and was drawing blood for routine tests.

'Her BP is still high, Nick,' she said. 'And she's absolutely certain of her dates.'

'Of course I am,' Melanie said. 'It only happened once. I don't need one of those scans to confirm anything. I don't even know what I'm doing here.' She pushed back the sheet covering her and swung her legs over the side of the bed, then stopped abruptly, closing her eyes.

'Dizzy?' Emma asked as she lifted her legs back onto the bed.

'A bit,' Melanie said.

'Why are you scared of having a scan, Melanie?' Nick asked gently.

'Don't know,' she said coldly. 'But I'm not having one and you can't make me.'

'Sweetheart, it's important we see what's going on with the baby. We don't know how long your blood pressure has been high and we need to check things out.' Nick's voice was soft, persuasive. Emma had forgotten just how persuasive he could be.

'Will it hurt?'

'No,' Emma said. 'Not at all. And you'll be able to see your baby on the screen.'

'Okay,' Melanie said.

The door opened and Audrey looked in. 'Sorry to interrupt,' she said. 'Emma, you're needed. Things are finally moving along with Carol.'

'I'll be right there,' Emma said. 'I'll be back, Melanie.'

She smiled at Melanie, then at Nick and hurried out of the room.

Things certainly were moving along with Carol. Her contractions were getting stronger, but her cervix was still only five centimetres dilated. She couldn't deliver the baby yet.

'I'm going to break your waters, Carol,' Emma said. 'You may feel a little discomfort, but it won't hurt. It's just another way to move things along.'

Nick walked in and smiled at Carol. 'Haven't you had that baby yet?' he said.

'I was waiting for you,' Carol quipped, then she gave a little sigh as Emma broke the membranes and there was a gush of fluid.

'It's clear,' Emma said. 'Let's hope this does the trick.'

It did, just as Emma hoped it would.

'I don't want you to push yet, Carol,' she said a short while later when Carol said she wanted to bear down. 'Will you breathe for me, please? Your cervix isn't quite ready. We don't want to rush this after waiting so long.'

There was no chance now of the baby turning. From that point on the delivery went without a hitch, and Emma called Ian to see the first glimpse of the baby as she emerged from the birth canal.

'It has black hair!' Ian reported, but Carol wasn't listening; she was in the throes of another contraction, and this one finished the delivery.

'A girl,' Emma said, laughing. 'And you were convinced it was a boy.'

Carol laughed and held out her arms. 'Know what?' she said. 'I don't care about being wrong. She's gorgeous.'

'She certainly is,' Emma agreed, still smiling. Days like this were what made her love her job. Handing a healthy baby to a well mother, what more could you ask? And to have Nick there beside

151

her, well that was just an added bonus. She turned to him and smiled and the look he gave her in return melted her insides. It wasn't a smile, more a smouldering wordless statement of intent.

6

The atmosphere was very different when Emma joined Nick after Carol's delivery for Melanie's scan. She could feel the tension in the room, but only because she was so in tune with Nick. His expression gave nothing away and his voice showed only mild concern, but Emma knew he was seriously worried.

'The baby is a little smaller than we'd expect at twenty-seven weeks,' he said.

'I told you,' Melanie cried. 'I know my dates. I'm not lying.'

'I'm not disputing your dates, sweetheart,' Nick said gently. 'The blood flow through the cord to the baby is intermittent. That explains why the size doesn't add up.'

'Can you do anything to make it grow?' Melanie asked tremulously.

'Well first we're going to try and

stabilise your blood pressure, and then we'll do another scan tomorrow. I don't want to rush in and deliver this baby too soon. Every day we can wait is a day closer to fewer problems for the baby.'

'I don't understand what all of this means,' Melanie said, her eyes flicking between Nick and Emma. 'What does it mean about the blood flow?'

Nick looked across at Emma and lifted his eyebrows slightly.

'Your baby relies on the cord for everything,' Emma told her. 'It's her life-support system if you like. Because the flow isn't steady, she isn't getting the oxygen and nutrients she needs. She needs amino acids in order to grow normally and with the intermittent blood flow through the cord, she's just not getting everything she should and it's affecting her growth.'

Melanie turned to look at the screen, blinking hard but unable to stop tears rolling down her face.

'I didn't think about it being real

before,' she wept. 'Not until I saw it up there on the screen. I don't want to lose this baby.'

'You won't,' Nick said with such assurance that even Emma believed him, despite knowing that the baby was only just borderline viable at the size she was. 'If we see no improvement tomorrow, we'll deliver by C-section, but we'll talk about that if it happens, okay?'

Melanie nodded.

'And in the meantime if you feel ill at all, you must tell someone. If you have a headache or blurred vision, in fact any discomfort or pain at all, I want you to report it immediately, no matter how trivial you may think it is. All right, Melanie?' Nick instructed. 'Okay? It's what we're here for, to look after you and the baby. Anything, anything at all troubling you and you just shout, okay? Promise me?'

She nodded again. She looked like a little girl, Emma thought, far younger than her eighteen years. But fear and vulnerability had that effect on people, made them appear to shrink in body and in age.

'We'll move you into a ward now,' Emma explained. 'You need plenty of rest and quiet.'

* * *

Once Melanie was settled, Emma joined Nick in the corridor to update him about Carol. While she was talking to him the end doors burst open yet again, and a group of people entered. Emma had a bad feeling about them right away. They gave off menacing vibes.

'Why have those doors been left unlocked?' Nick said angrily, striding towards them. There were four men and a woman, and Emma noticed John Logan behind them looking pale and worried. The men were all big and every one of them looked ready for a fight.

Nick wasn't in the least intimidated

by the group and didn't break his stride as they spread out across the corridor in front of him.

'Nick, be careful,' Emma whispered. If they decided to lay into him for whatever reason, no matter how tall and strong he was, he wouldn't be able to defend himself. Not only that, but she noticed at least two of the men had facial scarring which looked like old stab wounds. One of them had a purple line across his throat. These were men used to violence.

'What are you doing in here?' Nick demanded. He stood in the centre of the corridor, not exactly barring their way, but his presence seemed to erect an invisible barrier either side of him. 'How did you get in?'

'I let them in,' John said, stepping forward. He still looked dreadfully worried and rather shaken. 'I'm sorry, Nick.'

Emma hoped that Nick would realise as she had that his father had been intimidated into opening the door with his security code and to her relief, he seemed to.

'Not your fault, Dad,' he said, his voice softening somewhat. Then he turned back to the men in front of him. 'How dare you use force on an old man to gain entry here? Would you have tried your bullying tactics on a younger man? I think not!'

The men moved forward and one of them pushed into Nick, trying to edge him aside, but he refused to budge, standing his ground as solid as a brick wall.

'You're going nowhere,' he said, his voice unwavering. Emma wished she felt half as calm as he sounded. Her stomach had sunk to somewhere around her ankles and she felt herself trembling.

'Val, call security,' Nick said. 'And the police.'

At her desk and looking terrified, Val picked up the phone, her anxious eyes never leaving the scene playing out further along the corridor.

'If you won't leave, then I will have you forcibly removed,' Nick told the men. 'I don't kid myself that I can stop you all, but while we wait for the police to arrive you're welcome to try.'

Don't challenge them, Emma wanted to shout at him. But instead of taking up the challenge, the men backed down a little.

'There's no need for that,' the older of the men said. 'We're here to take Mel home. She shouldn't be in here. He shouldn't have brought her in.' He pointed accusingly at John.

'Nat, she's sick.' The woman who had come in with the men pushed herself forward. 'Her blood pressure's high. That can be dangerous in a pregnant woman.'

'She's expecting, she's not sick,' Nat snapped. 'Now, Doctor whatever your name is, let us through so we can get my daughter and then we'll leave.'

'All right,' Nick said, and Emma couldn't believe he was giving in so easily, but he hadn't moved to let them pass. 'But first you will listen to what I have to say, and then if you decide you still want to take her home, I won't try and stop you.'

'Make it quick,' Nat growled. 'I've got things to do.'

'Melanie has pregnancy-induced hypertension. If her blood pressure spikes it could bring on a seizure or a stroke, and that could happen at any time. At worst your daughter could die, and I haven't even started on the risks for the baby.'

'A stroke?' one of the younger men laughed. 'Old people have strokes. Melanie's just a kid.'

'Shut up!' Nat yelled at the younger man. Then he turned back to Nick. 'What? What risks?' he said, but it was clear that with those few words, Nick had reached him.

Emma heard doors opening and closing behind her and glanced over her shoulder to see several of the staff coming up behind them in support. At the other end of the corridor, two security men had arrived. She felt herself go weak with relief, but Nick had already got control over the situation.

'It's likely that we'll have to deliver the baby soon, and I mean within the next couple of days. If the baby survives she'll be on life support and could suffer respiratory disease and brain damage, and those are just two of the risks she will be facing. Now if you want to go ahead and take Melanie home now that you know exactly the kind of danger she faces, then go ahead, but I warn you by taking her now you are probably signing her and the baby's death warrants.'

Nick stepped aside and waited. The men shuffled, then the woman hit her husband between the shoulder blades, knocking him off balance.

'I told you, you idiot,' she yelled. 'I told you she was sick. And then you come here and start insulting the people who are looking after her. What's wrong with you?'

'Look,' Nick said, the anger gone from his voice. 'We're trying to stabilise

Melanie's blood pressure. She's scared enough as it is. You can go in and see her, but just for a couple of minutes so you can reassure yourselves she's okay. Then I'm going to have to ask you to leave.'

'Will you show us where to go, Doctor?' Melanie's mother asked.

'By all means,' Nick said. 'Come this way. I'll come in with you and answer any questions you may have. Just one thing — I haven't spoken to Melanie yet about the danger to her baby if we have to deliver. I don't want to worry her any more than necessary at this stage. Understood?'

They all nodded and murmured their agreement and made to follow him down the corridor.

'Just the parents,' he said. 'The rest of you can wait at the end. There are some chairs down there.'

He signalled to the security men that the situation was under control, but they chose to stick around, walking across to the desk and chatting with Val.

Emma was glad of their presence.

Nick showed them to Melanie's room, then left them alone for two minutes. He checked his watch as he came out.

'You all right?' he asked Emma. 'You've gone as white as a sheet. Do you want to go and sit down? I can get you a coffee or something.'

'I'm fine.' She gave him a wobbly smile. 'I was just a bit scared for you, that's all.'

'Scared for me?' he looked surprisingly pleased. 'Really?'

'Yes, Nick, really.' there was nothing wobbly about the smile she gave him now. 'I do care about what happens to you, you know.'

Nick leaned forward and for one heart-stopping moment she thought he was going to kiss her, but as his lips brushed her ear he whispered, 'If you're sure you're okay, would you take care of my father for me? He looks pretty shaken up, but that might be because I called him an old man. It'll take him a while to forgive me for that.'

He straightened up and grinned down at her, then his expression became serious again. 'I'm going back in,' he said. 'I want to make sure they don't say anything to upset that little lass.'

★　★　★

Emma looked at John and thought at once how ill he looked. He seemed to have aged quickly over the past five years. He was sitting on one of the plastic chairs in the corridor, looking as if his world had just collapsed about his ears.

'Are you all right, John?'

'A bit shaken,' he said with a nervous smile. 'I'll be all right.'

'I think there's more to it than that,' she murmured. 'Have you seen a doctor?'

'I *am* a doctor,' he said tetchily. 'And don't you start on that subject either; I get enough of it from Nick. I'm getting old, that's all, as my son so barbarically reminded me a few minutes ago.'

Emma stifled a laugh. Nick was right, his father had been insulted!

'I think Nick was just making a point,' she said, cocking her head on one side. 'Anyone can see you're not an old man, not by a long way.'

'You think?' he looked up at her. 'Well sometimes I feel it.' He got to his feet.

'Anyway, let me get you a coffee,' Emma said, taking his arm, which he wrenched away. She hadn't meant to insult him, but that seemed to be exactly what she'd done.

'I don't need a coffee and I don't need to sit down,' he said shortly. 'And let me remind you, I am senior to you here and I won't be spoken to like some sort of senile old fool.'

'John, I wouldn't dream . . . '

'Wouldn't you? You all seem to think because I'm semi-retired I must be past it,' he flashed, and then his eyes seemed to clear and he shook his head. 'I'm sorry, Emma. It's all been a bit of a strain. I shouldn't have let those people get the better of me and I certainly shouldn't be taking it out on you. Yes, I will have that coffee, thank you. And while I drink it you can tell me what you've been getting up to these past few years and you can tell me you forgive me for being an ungracious old fool.'

'You may have been ungracious, but you're not old,' Emma laughed and he grinned, his face taking on the familiar contours of the man she admired and liked so much. She led the way into her office and poured him a coffee, added two sugars and handed it to him.

'You even remember how I take my coffee.' He smiled gratefully. 'So, Emma, what have you been up to?'

'Oh, a bit of this and that,' she said evasively and his eyes narrowed.

'Why didn't you give Nick a chance to explain?' he asked, his question catching her off guard. 'I know he was wrong, and God knows I tell him so every chance I get, but you must have known he was looking for you.'

'He didn't look for me,' she said. 'He went to Australia.'

'Where did you get that idea?' John frowned. 'Nick cancelled his plans when he found you'd gone. He searched for you and every time he got back here, he went and pestered your poor aunt asking for news. It was almost as if her house became his centre and he had to touch base every time he got back.'

Emma felt a jolt, as if she'd had an electric shock. If she and Nick had talked, then she'd always felt they might have resolved things. As it was, she thought that he'd rushed off to live in another country and he thought she was deliberately avoiding him.

'I don't think that's possible,' she said, her mouth suddenly dry. 'Aunt Rose knew where I was. She would have told me if Nick was looking for me.'

She broke off. Would Aunt Rose have told her? John was looking steadily at her. Gone was the old, frail-looking man. How could she ever have thought him vulnerable? He was probably right, and it was just the shock of what had happened when the travellers forced him to open the door. Right now he looked as sharp as he ever had.

'Would she?' he asked. 'Are you sure about that, Emma? If things had been right between you, and if my son had gone about asking you to go to Australia with him in a different way, would you have gone?'

'I don't know,' she replied truthfully. 'I would certainly have given it serious thought.'

She knew what John was saying. She and Rose were very close. It would have broken Rose's heart if Emma had gone to live abroad. And it wasn't just that. It was the revelation that Nick had stayed, that he'd given up everything to look for her.

'Please, John,' she said, her eyes dark with pain. 'Don't tell Nick we had this conversation. He didn't tell me that he cancelled his plans to go to Australia. I assumed he'd been and come back.'

'Does knowing this change anything?' John asked.

'No,' she said, staring at her hands which were clasping each other as if her life depended on it. 'If anything, it makes things worse.'

She looked up at him, eyes deep with sorrow. Now if she told Nick about Keira and Daisy he would believe that she'd withheld her pregnancy from him out of spite.

'Please, John.'

'I won't say a word.' He sighed, getting to his feet. 'But I think you're a pair of fools. You loved each other then and I suspect you love each other still, but if you're going to let pride or whatever it is get in your way, then you're even bigger idiots than I thought you were. Life's too short for this, Emma, much too short. You have to grab your chances for happiness while you can.' He left the office, closing the door behind him.

Emma buried her face in her hands. All that time she'd been missing Nick, wanting him, wanting him to know about their babies . . . and he'd been looking for her. And the one person she trusted above all others hadn't told her.

'Oh, Aunt Rose,' she wept. 'Why?'

★ ★ ★

Rose and Keira were out in the garden when she got home from the hospital, a little late because she'd become involved in a delivery just before shift change and had wanted to see it through. She'd also looked in on Jenny and Melanie before leaving. It helped remind her that no matter how bad she might think her problems were, she still had Keira.

Rose was sitting in a garden chair while Keira knelt on the grass surrounded by a long daisy chain she'd been making. 'Mummy!' she yelled, leaping to her feet and running into her arms in a haze of sweet-smelling grass and the scent of daisies.

'Hello, love,' Rose said and her smile was so warm, so welcoming that Emma's heart broke all over again. It was so out of character for Rose to have lied to Nick. She must have been dreadfully desperate to have done it. And being angry with her now would change nothing. While Keira went back to her daisy chain, Emma went to Rose and hugged her.

'What was that for?'

'Just . . . I love you,' Emma said with a self-conscious little laugh. 'And I don't think I've ever told you that or how grateful I am for all you've done for me.'

'Oh, there,' Rose blushed. 'What's brought all this on?'

Emma licked her lips. 'I know that Nick didn't go away,' she said, having already decided on the way home that she was going to have this conversation with her aunt. 'Not to Australia anyway.'

Rose's eyes filled with fear and she flashed a look at Keira, but Keira was too far away from them and too lost in

171

her own little world to hear what they were saying.

'I know that he came here looking for me.'

Rose closed her eyes and groaned. 'I knew you'd find out one day,' she whispered and to Emma's astonishment, tears began to roll down her aunt's face. 'I've dreaded this day for so long. Please try to understand why I did it, Emma. I didn't want you to go so far away. I thought I'd lose you forever and I couldn't bear that. But believe me when I say that a day hasn't passed since Keira was born that I didn't regret what I did with all my heart — but by then it was too late; the damage was done. You thought he'd abandoned you, he thought you'd done the same, and it would have all come out that it was my fault. You would never have forgiven me . . . and I don't see how you can now.'

Emma hugged her again, eager to show her that it made no difference. There had been too much pain and heartache and she didn't want to add to it.

'And then Nick stopped coming here,' Rose went on, keen now to get it all off her chest. 'Keira had been born by then and I told him that you'd made a new life for yourself and assumed he would do the same. I thought I'd left it too late to make amends. Oh, Emma, if you knew how sorry I am, how haunted I've been. I've wanted to make amends, to put things right, but I've been so afraid.'

'I do know,' Emma said. 'But that's the last secret between us, Aunt Rose. I don't want there ever to be anything like this between us again.'

'Nor do I,' Rose said with a shudder. 'It's been hell living with that all this time. I was so afraid that when you found out you'd hate me, because if you hated me half as much as I hated myself I couldn't bear it.'

'I couldn't hate you, Aunt Rose,' Emma said warmly. 'Not in a million years.'

'You don't understand,' Rose said, her voice heavy with regret. 'He really was desperate to find you. He made me promise to tell you that he was looking for you.'

Emma had guessed that much and that was what made it all so much worse. When Nick found out about Keira and Daisy, as he surely must, then he would believe that Emma had deliberately shut him out of their lives. He would never forgive her for that.

'Water under the bridge,' Emma said, more cheerfully than she felt. Then she went to join Keira, who was kneeling on the grass threading the daisy stems through each other.

'I'm making a daisy chain for Daisy,' Keira said. 'Can we put it on her grave?'

Emma nodded. She was too choked to speak and deep down she was angry with Rose, but she knew it was a negative emotion and giving way to it would solve nothing.

* * *

In the morning Emma arrived at the hospital just as John and Nick were pulling into the car park. They exchanged greetings, then fell into step with each other and walked in together. Nick smiled at her and her heart turned over, but instead of soaring it felt like a brick in her chest.

She knew she would have to tell him about their twins, and soon; and that things would never be the same between them. She could never betray Rose and tell Nick that she'd lied to him. Rose had enough on her conscience without that.

'We were just discussing Melanie,' John said. 'Nick has agreed that I should take over her care, at least for today. If I have to go ahead with a C-section, I'd like you there, Emma.'

'Thank you,' Emma said, warmed. 'I'd like to be there.'

'Good.' John smiled then stepped back so that Emma and Nick could walk through the doors into the hospital side by side.

'It's embarrassing the way he's trying to push us together,' Nick whispered when his father had spotted a colleague he needed to speak to. 'Although I must say, the thought of being pushed together with you is a very nice one.'

'I'm just going to see Michael,' John called out. 'I'll be five minutes.'

Emma and Nick turned in the opposite direction. Emma kept her face turned away from Nick so that he wouldn't see the tell-tale flush in her cheeks.

'I lied to you, Emma. I said I didn't like what was happening to me — to us — but I lied. I do like it — rather too much; and I think you do too,' Nick said so softly she barely heard him.

'Excuse me?' she said.

They stopped walking and turned to face each other. He put his hands on her shoulders and they both felt the jolt. She wanted him to kiss her right there in the hospital, in front of everyone. She didn't care what people thought! She loved him. She swayed a little before gaining control of her leaping senses and told herself firmly that this could, *must* not, be.

'What we had, I know it was a long time ago, but I think it's worth reviving — and I know you feel the same way too. The way you respond to my touch, the way you look at me. Don't tell me I'm wrong here, Emma. For my part, God, I ache for you, all the damn time. I couldn't believe my luck when you walked back into my life.'

'Nick, I . . . '

'No,' he said, pressing his finger against her lips. 'Just think about what I said. I'm asking for another chance and this time, I won't let you down or hurt you, I swear. I've changed. I know a lot of guys say that, but in my case it's true. I've had five years to think about the mistakes I made, five years of bitter regret, and it's changed me; and I think — I hope — I'm a better man.'

The worst of it was, she believed him. But she was going to have to hurt him, she knew it, and she wasn't sure he'd still feel the same way about her when she had.

'There's something you have to know,' she said at last, her heart thumping painfully against her ribs. 'Something about me, about us. It may change the way you feel about me; in fact I'm certain it will. We really need to talk, Nick.'

But here wasn't the place and this certainly wasn't the time, and she hated herself for the look of hope she'd put in his beautiful soft eyes.

'I can't imagine anything you could have done that would change the way I feel, Emma. But okay, tonight?' he asked. 'Dinner? My place? I'll make lasagne.'

She nodded. Aunt Rose wouldn't mind baby-sitting; she was almost as keen for Emma to sort all this out as Emma herself. And the talking was essential. The kissing and all the rest of it was better than good, it was wonderful; and she wanted that as much as he did. But the talking had to be done. The past had to be ironed out properly before they could even think about taking their relationship any further. If he still wanted to once he knew.

'Are you still . . . ?' she began.

'No, I moved out of the flat,' he said and the hopeful look was still there, the look that seemed to say he expected her to stay the night, stay forever maybe, the look she would have to remove before the night was over. 'I've got a house now. Once I decided to stay here and put down roots, I got the house.'

For the wife and children he wanted to have one day? Emma wondered. For her if she came back?

'Sorry about that, children,' John said jovially as he joined them and placed a hand on each of their shoulders. 'You weren't waiting for me, were you?' He looked from one to the other then dropped his hands. 'I'm sorry, I've interrupted something,' he said contritely. 'Would you like me to make myself scarce?'

'Dad . . . ' Nick began with an embarrassed smile that brought out the deep dimples in his cheeks.

'All right, point taken,' John said airily. 'Let's just get to work, shall we?'

'You're keen today, Dad,' Nick said with a smile as his father hurried on ahead of them. 'Actually, it's good to see him so enthused,' Nick lowered his voice to speak to Emma and confided, 'I've been a little worried about him lately. I think he does too much and overtires himself.'

'I thought yesterday when he came in with Melanie's family that he seemed rather . . . ' She struggled to find the right word.

'Feeble?' Nick provided wryly.

'No, I'd never say that about him. He's a strong man, a very capable one.'

'He was,' Nick said, his concern obvious. 'It doesn't seem to take much to rattle him these days.'

It was so easy to talk to Nick, and so nice. It was awful knowing that soon she would have to ruin all that. Nick was sure to want to see Keira and he would remain civil with Emma for that reason, but Emma would have to prepare their little girl first.

It occurred to her that Keira would also have a grandpa. After she told Nick about their child tonight, Keira's close family would effectively double.

7

Once on the ward, Emma found herself thrust straight in on a difficult delivery. Kellie, the midwife on duty, stayed for a while, but it was clear she was almost as exhausted as the mother and a fresh pair of hands was required.

'It's been a mad night,' Kellie said tiredly. 'I'd say almost frantic. Do you mind if I slip away now? I don't think I'm going to be much help to you here.'

'Go,' Emma said with a smile. 'Would you like me to let you know the outcome of this?'

'Oh, please. Just text me. All I want to know is whether it's a boy or girl giving us all this trouble. I think it's going to end up an assisted delivery though. She's had just about enough. However, I tried talking to them about assisting and they're both adamant they can do this without any help. Him mainly, but he's not the one lying there suffering!'

Emma nodded. Lucy, the young mother, looked all in, and her partner Kris standing beside her was clutching her hand, looking fit to drop. Emma had met Lucy just a few days ago when she'd come in for an antenatal check and thought she was a prime candidate for a trouble-free delivery. But you couldn't always get it right.

'Let's see what a fresh pair of hands can do,' Emma said brightly and Lucy looked up at her and smiled.

'We're glad you're here,' she panted. 'At least you seemed to understand when I talked to you about wanting a natural birth.'

'In an ideal world it's what we'd all like,' Emma said. 'But sometimes nature needs a helping hand. But let's see what happens. We need a couple of really good pushes from you now, Lucy, as much strength as you can put into it.'

The next contraction came and Lucy tried, tried so very hard, but her pushing was at best half-hearted and it had nothing to do with her will. It was lack of physical strength and sheer exhaustion controlling this labour now.

'I don't think I can.' Lucy's voice shook. 'It's so hard.'

'You can do it,' Lucy's partner urged. 'Come on, Lucy, breathe, breathe, and remember what we said.'

'Oh shut up!' Lucy screamed as she was gripped by another contraction. 'Just clear off and stop telling me what to do! What the hell do you know about pain?'

'Let's have a really good push now, Lucy,' Emma urged, stifling a smile when she saw the hurt, baffled expression on the father-to-be's face. He had it coming to him, really, and Lucy was letting him have it with both barrels. Strangely enough, yelling at her partner seemed to add a little to the power of her pushes, but it still wasn't enough.

'Come on now, push. That's great, you can do it,' Emma encouraged with the next contraction.

'Come on, darling,' Kris said, finally daring to speak again. 'Push . . . push.'

Emma checked the monitor. The baby was showing no sign of distress, but that situation could quickly change and all the pushing was getting Lucy precisely nowhere except more and more exhausted. Right now, Emma's biggest concern was the mother. She'd already been pushing for well over an hour and she seemed to have used up all her strength. The outburst had only revived her a little and now her energy was sapped more than ever.

At the next contraction, again there was no progress. Emma looked at the clock. Each contraction simply served to drain Lucy further and it wasn't a situation that was going to improve.

'Lucy, we're going to have to help you a little here,' Emma said, preparing herself for an argument. 'Did Kellie discuss an assisted delivery with you at all?'

'No.' Lucy's eyes widened with fear and she squeezed her partner's hand

and looked at him.

'We want as natural a birth as possible,' he said, but he didn't look very convinced. 'We were going to use the birthing pool, but the other midwife said that it wasn't possible. The last thing we want is Lucy's legs up in stirrups and the baby being pulled out with forceps.'

Lucy screamed, a raw animal sound that tore itself out of her throat.

'Do something,' Kris cried, rapidly changing his mind as Lucy's scream seemed to go on and on. 'Do what you have to do, but do something.'

How quickly he had changed from the encouraging partner to a man in the grip of panic.

Emma turned to Audrey. 'Would you ask Nick to come in, please? Tell him I need his help with a ventouse delivery.'

'This isn't what we wanted,' Kris said tearfully as Audrey hurried out.

'It isn't what *you* wanted, Kris,' Lucy yelled. Her face was red and soaked with sweat and tears. 'But it's not you doing this — it's me, and it hurts . . . oh God, how it hurts!'

'You can help by mopping her face,' Emma told him. 'At least you can help her to feel a little more comfortable. Lucy, I'm going to have to put your legs up in supports and we'll drop the end of the bed.' She took a moment to smile at Kris. 'We won't be using forceps,' she said. 'Lucy, we're going to use the ventouse. Do you know what that means?'

Lucy sobbed and nodded. 'Yes, but please do it quickly.'

'We're still going to need you to push when the time comes, but we'll be helping you and it will be much easier for you.'

'Hi, Lucy,' Nick said as he walked in followed by June. The cavalry! 'I hear you need a little help in here.'

'Doctor Logan,' Lucy wailed. 'Am I glad to see you.' She didn't say more as another contraction took hold. Nick monitored this one and agreed that Emma had made the right call at the right time. The baby was going nowhere without help and according to the monitor his heartbeat was becoming erratic.

Nick flashed Emma a look and smiled, and her insides melted. Then it was all systems go. Ventouse was a much less invasive procedure than forceps and carried far less risk to the mother.

'I'm going to put this cap on the baby's head,' Nick explained as he showed the parents the soft plastic cap which looked like a small sink plunger. 'Then I'll apply suction, which will take a few minutes. The one thing I should warn you is that the baby's head will look a little strange after delivery, but it's really nothing to worry about and will return to normal after a few days.'

'We can do this without an episiotomy,' Emma said, and Nick nodded his agreement. It was yet another advantage of using the ventouse instead of forceps. He worked quickly to place the suction cap on the baby's head. Emma had seen this done a lot of times and she'd also seen the cap pulled off by an over-eager doctor. If it happened too many times then the ventouse had to be abandoned and forceps used instead, but she had every faith in Nick that he would get this absolutely right.

Emma and June took up a station on each leg and Audrey took hold of Lucy's other hand.

'The pump will be noisy,' Nick said. 'Everybody ready?'

While Nick applied the suction, Emma talked to Lucy about what would happen next.

'When the cap is firmly in place, we'll ask you to push when you get a contraction, but instead of doing all the work alone, you'll be getting that bit of extra help you need.'

'How many times will I have to push?' Lucy whimpered.

'Three at the most,' Emma said.

'Two.' Nick grinned and he winked at Emma. 'At the most.'

He was probably right. In his expert

hands the birth should proceed quickly, but not too quickly, Emma thought. Experienced doctors knew that patience and gentle pulling got better results than the kind of physical force required with forceps. And it would be far more comfortable afterwards for the baby.

After several minutes, Nick said that they were ready to go. The cap was firmly in place on the baby's head and Lucy could push with her next contraction.

'That's great, Lucy,' Emma said when she started to push. This time Lucy didn't scream but put every ounce of her energy into pushing her baby into the world because now she knew she only had to do this a couple more times. 'You're doing really well, keep it going, keep pushing.'

'Go Lucy!' June joined in. 'Good girl, good girl! We're really getting somewhere now.'

Kris had fallen silent now. He was still clutching Lucy's hand, but he was watching the birth, goggled-eyed with wonder. At last the baby was on the move.

'Would you like to feel your baby's head, Lucy?' Nick asked and gently guided her hand down. Her eyes widened, this time with awe and she burst out laughing. Nick looked at her partner, 'Kris? Come and say hi to your baby.'

Kris came down and had a look and immediately burst into tears.

'Good man,' Nick murmured softly with real understanding, real feeling and Emma thought again what a wonderful father he would be given the chance.

Emma placed a towel on Lucy's stomach and noticed that Jimmy had quietly entered the room with Wendy, one of the paediatricians. They were always on hand for an assisted delivery.

'For the baby,' Emma smiled as she smoothed out the towel. 'Who will be here very, very soon.'

During the next contraction Nick again pulled gently, his eyes sharp with concentration — eyes that changed in an instant from unwavering focus to joy. He removed the cap and handed the baby to Jimmy, leaving Emma to deliver the placenta while Wendy quickly checked the baby. Less than two minutes later, Lucy was holding her baby while a very joyful Kris was taking photographs.

'We want one of the team, Kris,' Lucy said and insisted that they all pose for the camera. Jimmy had gone and Kris arranged them so that Nick was standing at the back towering over Emma, June and Audrey. He was standing right behind Emma; she could feel his body brushing lightly against hers.

I shouldn't be having these kinds of thoughts, Emma told herself, but these kinds of thoughts were far too nice to let go. And after tonight, she'd be lucky if Nick wanted to touch her with a bargepole.

★ ★ ★

So what was it she'd done or thought she'd done that was so terrible? Nick wondered. There was no blemish on her work record, so it must be personal.

He took one last look at the baby. The skull was hardly out of shape at all. He'd seen some babies born with the help of ventouse end up with heads shaped like ice-cream cones. And there was no evidence of cephalhaematoma, the blood blister which could be an unsightly but not dangerous side-effect of ventouse delivery. All in all it had been a good morning's work, and his only wish was that all deliveries could be as easy as this one.

He said his goodbyes and left the delivery suite to get cleaned up before going to catch up on some paperwork. As he walked down the corridor, he saw his father coming out of one of the side rooms.

'Busy morning?' John asked, still in his happy mood. He wasn't a miserable man by any means, but it was unusual to see him quite so buoyed up. There was a bounce in his step as he walked along and a smile on his face.

'What's happened, Dad?' Nick asked.

'I have no idea,' John said. 'I just feel so alive, I suppose; as if I have purpose again. And I'm very happy with my life. Sometimes we should stop and take stock and learn to appreciate what we have.'

'That's exactly what I'm hoping to do, Dad,' Nick said.

'I'm on my way to talk to Emma now,' John went on. 'I'm planning on having another look at Melanie in an hour. But I've been thinking, would you rather handle this, so that you and Emma can work together?'

Crafty old fox! 'I'd like nothing more, but I have clinic later and from what I've seen of Melanie's obs, she's going to require intervention sooner rather than later. Of course I could cancel clinic.'

'No need,' John said and carried on his way. Nick heard him whistling. It was good to see him like that, full of cheer again.

★ ★ ★

'Hold the needles in whichever way feels comfortable,' Emma said as Jenny tried to get to grips with two knitting needles. 'And relax — your fingers are very tense. Loosen your grip a little. Remember this is just practice; it doesn't matter if you drop a stitch and it's supposed to help you relax, not make you tense up.'

'You make it look so easy,' Jenny muttered. 'But I would like to learn to knit. It would be nice to be able to knit some little garments, if not for these two, then for any more babies I might have. I don't want these to be the only children I have.' She laid the needles down on her lap and sighed.

Emma could hardly stop herself from laughing out loud. That was the first time she'd heard Jenny talk as if she was going to have these children safely. One giant leap for positive thought.

Despite what she'd said about being all fingers and thumbs, and after a little initial awkwardness, Jenny proved to be a quick learner. She held the needles in a way that made Emma want to wrestle them out of her hands and show her how to hold them properly, but she was the one who'd told her to be comfortable about it.

'I've done a whole row,' Jenny said proudly. 'Well I can hardly believe it. Thank you for showing me, Emma. What do I do now? Just keep on going? I can't believe how quickly it grows.'

As Emma had hoped, it was proving to be a calming distraction for Jenny, who had thus far had trouble settling to anything.

'Knitting?' Nick laughed as he walked in.

'Therapy,' Jenny laughed back at him. 'Emma taught me how to do this. Look, I've done a whole row all by myself.'

'Excellent,' Nick said, then added with a mischievous twinkle in his eye, 'If I'd known you were a knitter, Emma, I'd have asked you to make me a sweater.'

'Oh, Emma knits for the preemie

babies,' Jenny said merrily.

'Does she indeed?' Nick gave Emma a look.

It was nothing unusual. A lot of nurses, particularly in their line, knitted for the preemies.

'Goodness,' Emma said, getting abruptly to her feet. 'Is that the time? My break is over. Sorry, Jenny, but I'm going to have to run. Excuse me.'

She hurried from the room. It was only a bit of knitting, for goodness sake, she told herself frantically as she dashed down towards the desk. Didn't give anything away. Certainly didn't require this almost-run kind of walk that could result in twisted ankles and silly accidents.

She forced herself to slow down and was almost knocked over by Nick, who was coming up fast behind and walked right into the back of her. 'Hey, what's the hurry?' he said lazily. 'Didn't you hear me calling you?'

It would have been nigh impossible to hear anything over the pounding in her ears, Emma thought. 'What did you want me for?' She was aware that there were other staff members hanging about, watching them.

'Knitting,' he said, laughing. 'I still can't believe it. The Emma I used to know wouldn't have had time in her life for knitting.'

'Things change,' she said. 'Was there anything else?'

'The lasagne,' he said, lowering his voice and smiling at the reaction of those watching. They seemed to lean towards them as if hoping to catch what he said.

'What about it?' Emma whispered back, laughing despite herself.

'Are you all right with beef, or would you prefer vegetarian?'

'I'd prefer the vegetarian option,' she said and without thinking went on, 'I usually do vegetarian food at home because K . . . '

The first letter of her daughter's name stuck in her throat and almost choked her. Meanwhile Nick was looking down at her, his head slightly on one side, a curious expression on his face.

'Because?' he lifted his eyebrows.

How could she tell him that his daughter was a vegetarian and it was easier to join her than to cook two different meals? Well she almost had!

'Because . . . ' she hesitated, then inspiration struck. 'Cooking vegetarian food is simpler, easier, I guess.'

'You don't sound very sure.' He frowned, but it was laced with humour.

'I don't think I'm very sure of anything right now.' She gave a short, embarrassed laugh and turned to walk away. The curious were still staring and looking disappointed, but Nick called out behind her and gave them all what they were waiting for.

'I can't wait until tonight, Emma!'

She blushed furiously, noted the smiles surrounding her, and carried on her way, blushing even more deeply when she passed Val who murmured, 'Go girl!' as she went by.

'My dear, the blood flow to the baby has decreased further,' John said softly when he and Emma did Melanie's second scan. 'That means we must deliver her immediately. Now under normal circumstances, your body would secrete steroid hormones which ready the baby for life outside the womb. In your case this will not happen, so we will administer betamethasone, which will help the baby's lungs to mature.'

Melanie looked from one to the other of them. 'I don't understand.'

'What I'm saying is that we're going to give your baby all the help we can to survive after delivery. Even so, it's going to be a bumpy ride for her and she will require specialist care in our Neonatal Intensive Care Unit.'

At that moment, right on cue, the door opened and Jimmy breezed in with Wendy and two neonatal nurses.

'And these people are the team from the Neonatal Intensive Care Unit who will be taking responsibility for baby as soon as she is born,' John went on, and he introduced each one of them by name just as he had the rest of the team. He knew them all by name, but then he'd picked each one of them specially for this operation. It was going to be so delicate, so dangerous, that he had to know he had the best help available. Emma felt absolutely honoured to be included on that team.

Jimmy glanced at the screen, then smiled warmly at Melanie. 'We will have to rush her away pretty quickly once she's born,' he told her. 'But she won't be very far away. We're right next door so as soon as you're able to after the delivery, you can come along and see her. They'll bring you along in a wheelchair just as soon as they can.'

'You keep calling it a 'her',' Melanie said. She was still looking from one face to another, searching for something.

'I call all our babies here girls and I get it right about half the time,' John chuckled. Then he became serious again. 'So are you all straight, Melanie? Do you have any questions?'

Melanie shook her head. Emma knew how she felt. Frightened. Bewildered. She reached out and squeezed Melanie's hand. Not to mention overwhelmed by all these strange faces. But at least she was seeing them all for the first time without masks. Hopefully it would make it less intimidating for her once the C-section was underway. 'It will be all right,' she promised.

'Will you be there?'

'I'll be with you the whole time,' Emma said. 'I won't leave you. But right now, Jimmy will just talk to you about what to expect after the baby is born. She's all yours, Jimmy.'

He smiled a dazzling smile and moved forward. Wendy often left it to him to speak to the mothers. He had such a way of putting people at ease that it was too good a skill not to make frequent use of.

'Hello, Mel.' He explained to her exactly what to expect. Emma thought you would never imagine that this baby was in any trouble at all.

While Jimmy was talking to Melanie, John pulled Emma aside. 'Melanie is showing significant proteinuria and her BP is 160/100. We don't just have PIH, now we have pre-eclampsia, and I am seriously concerned for her health. We have to move quickly. As soon as Jimmy has finished with the pep talk, we're all systems go. And twenty . . . ' He faltered. 'What?' He shook his hand and stared at it, puzzled.

'John, are you okay?' Emma asked.

'Strange,' he murmured, then smiled. 'We have to move quickly.'

'John, wait,' Emma whispered. 'Are you feeling okay? If you're not feeling well, we can . . . '

'I'm feeling fine,' he said with a grin. 'What's all the fuss about?'

Emma looked around. No one else had heard their exchange, but she had a bad feeling about this. Should she tell anyone? She looked at John closely. He looked fine. Perhaps the alarm bells were unnecessary and Tom the registrar was going to be on the team if anything happened.

Not that anything is going to happen, she told herself.

*   *   *

It brought back memories watching John at work, and swept away any worries Emma might have had. She had always admired his skill and his patience. He made a perfect incision and set to work, wasting no time in delivering the baby, which turned out to be a girl as he had predicted.

Emma felt a stab of trepidation when she saw her. So tiny, and much smaller than either of her twins had been. She wasn't even shown to Melanie before Jimmy whisked her away. Gone was the ever-present cheerful expression on Jimmy's face, and in its place a face set in grim determination.

'I was right.' John beamed. 'You have a daughter.'

'A little girl,' Melanie whispered. 'Thank you. Is she all right?'

She wasn't breathing, but Wendy Hibbard the paediatric consultant was intubating her right there before moving her to the NICU. Before the team from NICU left, Jimmy turned and gave Emma a stiff smile and a thumbs-up.

'It's not looking at all bad, Melanie,' Emma said. 'She's over the first hurdle.'

'Her name is Paige,' Melanie said, voice trembling with emotion.

Emma didn't mention that little Paige had a whole field of hurdles to jump before she would be home and dry. She smiled down at Melanie while John finished off, but it seemed to be taking an awful long time.

'Sir . . . ' Tom said. 'John . . . ' And something in his voice rang alarm bells.

Emma looked over at John and did a double take. He looked dazed. His hands were shaking and a film of sweat had formed across his brow. How long had he been standing there like that? Something strange, too, about one of his eyes.

'Sir, please, let me take over here.'

But John made no move. Tom shot Emma a frantic look. 'Get him out of the way,' he said urgently.

'John,' Emma said, concern for both him and Melanie rising up, swamping her.

'BP's dropping,' Helen, the anaesthetist, shouted.

Emma saw Melanie's eyes roll back.

'John,' she called out again, and while the anaesthetist struggled to save Melanie and Tom tried to get near enough to take over, Emma ran to John's side and pulled him out of the way. 'John, what's wrong?'

'What?' He swayed, then looked down at the blood on his gloved hands as if he'd been taken by surprise.

Emma turned from him and ran back to the bed.

'Asystole,' Helen said gravely. 'Emma, take care of John. We'll take it from here.'

Emma took one last look at the flat-line on the heart monitor and turned back to John as he was sliding to the floor. As she ran to him she heard Helen shock Melanie.

'John!' she knelt down beside him and kept his head from striking the floor. How could this be happening? He was so well this morning. Almost too well. The doors flew open and the crash team came in. More help for Melanie, but no one seemed to be coming to help John. Emma cradled his head in her arms and felt helpless as she listened to the battle to save Melanie's life.

All she could think was that she'd promised to stay with her and now she'd left her side, left her surrounded by strangers, torn between wanting to be there with her and not wanting to abandon John.

He was conscious, trying to speak, but unable to move. Emma knew what had happened as he looked up at her. It wasn't just a faint, nor a mere dizzy spell; John had had a full-blown stroke. The whole of the right side of his face had lost all elasticity and drooped down. His mouth was pulled down at the corner and a thin trickle of saliva ran down his chin. His right arm hung at his side, lifeless and limp. He was like a puppet with half his strings cut.

The episode earlier that had started the alarm bells ringing had been a transient ischaemic attack. How could she have missed that?

'Some help here!' she yelled across at the team who were surrounding Melanie and as she yelled, they all stepped back from the bed, heads hanging.

'That's it,' Tom said. 'We've got her back.'

'This man needs help, now!' Emma shouted. And where the hell was Nick? 'Hang in there, John,' she said. 'Help's coming. You're going to be okay.'

A trolley was brought in and John was carefully lifted onto it and taken away. Emma made to follow. She wanted to go with John. She didn't want to leave him like that, but everyone was moving so fast. She stumbled out of the theatre and found herself in the corridor, where she ran into Nick. He grabbed her arm.

'What in God's name is going on, Emma?' he said. 'Where are you going? You know damn well you don't wander round out here in that state.'

She looked down at herself. She was covered in blood. Melanie's blood. And then she looked up at him and realised he didn't know. He didn't know anything about what had happened.

'Nick . . . Oh, Nick . . . ' she whispered, but he was propelling her back through the door, out of sight.

'Melanie's family are out there, for God's sake. You don't want them to see you looking like that, and I sure as hell don't want any of my patients seeing you wandering round looking like some kind of butcher.'

'Melanie crashed, Nick,' Tom said dully. 'We almost lost her. She's still in a bad way. And I'm so sorry about your father.'

'My father?'

Emma came to her senses. Nick was right; it was no use her stumbling round in a state of shock. She had to get a grip. There was no easy way to tell him, so she just came out with it.

'Your father just had a stroke, Nick.'

'A what? Dad?' Nick gaped at her, then laughed. 'But that's impossible. And what do you mean Melanie almost died? We don't damn well lose women during C-sections, and my father certainly doesn't.' He paled.

'It wasn't his fault, Nick,' Emma said, reading his thoughts, knowing exactly what would be going through his mind.

'Fault? What are you implying?'

'I'm not implying anything,' Emma said, but before she had chance to explain, Nick had rushed off to see his father. That still left Melanie's family.

'We'd better get cleaned up, Tom,' Emma said, her voice flat. 'Then we'd better speak to Melanie's family.'

8

It was raining as Emma drove into the village — a hard, steady rain. Her date with Nick, if it could be called that, had been called off. Apart from the fact that it wouldn't be appropriate, Nick was keeping vigil at his father's bedside in the stroke unit that was attached to the Bob.

She got out of the car, locked it and ran to her front door. Rose and Keira were sitting snuggled up together on the sofa, watching a movie on television. As always, Keira leapt up and greeted her with hugs and smiles. Tonight Emma held her extra tight and for rather longer than usual.

'Watch the film and tell me what happens, Keira,' Rose said, seeing that Emma was disturbed. 'Mummy can come in the kitchen with me and I'll make her some tea.'

Once in the kitchen, Rose turned to Emma, her face etched with concern. 'What happened?'

'We almost lost a young mother today,' Emma said wearily. 'She's little more than a kid herself, and it's still touch and go. She's very poorly. And Nick's father had a stroke. A pretty big one.'

She didn't want to elaborate further. Didn't want to think about cradling that poor man's head in her arms; didn't want to think about Melanie's young, frail body hanging in the balance while her baby fought for her life in the NICU. She didn't want to think about any of it, but it kept flashing through her mind. She kept seeing Melanie's mother, her face crumpling in on itself as she sank to the floor when told the news. And the father, Nat, the big tough guy, falling to his knees beside his wife and weeping like a baby. Two people literally knocked off their feet by grief.

'Don't give up on her,' Emma had

told them. 'She can come through this.'

'But what if she doesn't?' Melanie's mother had replied.

'I'm so sorry,' Rose said. 'The poor girl and poor Nick. It must have been an awful shock for him.'

'Yes, I'm sure it was,' Emma said stiffly.

A shock for him, but was it her fault? Should she have listened to those alarm bells and made the fuss she'd been too afraid to make? And if she was going to admit feelings like that to herself, did that mean that some part of her somewhere thought that John was to blame for what happened to Melanie? It wasn't some thing she wanted to contemplate — blaming someone for something like that; apportioning guilt. It was dangerous ground. And if anyone was to blame, then surely it was her for ignoring her instincts.

★ ★ ★

'Have you come to see our little Paige?' Jimmy said when Emma walked into the NICU the next morning.

She nodded. She'd hardly slept a wink all night thinking about this little girl. Who would take care of her if Melanie didn't rally? What would become of her? She'd just come from the intensive care unit where Melanie's dad was sitting vigil.

'I keep talking to her,' he said. 'I've told her all about the baby.'

'That's good,' Emma said. 'That's the best thing you can do.'

'Doreen thinks it's pointless,' he said. 'She thinks she's already gone.'

'She hasn't,' Emma said. 'Melanie's still there.'

And there was the little baby in the incubator — a tiny, skinny little thing covered in tubes and wires, her pathetic little body vibrating.

'Is it all right if I come in?' a voice said and she turned to see Melanie's mother behind her. Her eyes were red from crying. She was convinced they

214

were going to lose Melanie, but she had hope in this struggling infant.

'Of course, please come in,' Emma said, moving aside.

'Hello, Doctor,' she said to Jimmy and he didn't correct her, just smiled kindly. 'How is she?'

'She's a fighter,' Jimmy said. Then he flashed a look at Emma. 'Like her mum.'

Doreen crept slowly forward, almost as if she was afraid to look at her grandchild, and when he saw her look of concern Jimmy quickly said, 'The reason for the vibration is because of the high frequency of the ventilator. It looks alarming, but it's quite normal. She's had a little trouble with her blood pressure and we've stabilised her. She weighs in at one pound six ounces, which is a pretty good weight all things considered, and she's a fraction under a foot long.'

Doreen nodded her thanks then turned to Emma. 'You were with my daughter when it happened, weren't you?'

'Yes, I was,' Emma said, her breath

catching in her throat because when Melanie had crashed and they'd fought to bring her back, she had been kneeling on the floor with John Logan.

'That's what the doctor told us. He said she was never on her own.'

'Not for a minute,' Emma said fiercely, because that much was true. No one could have worked harder to save Melanie than those people did yesterday.

'Did she say anything before she . . . you know . . . ?'

She and Tom had already told Doreen all of this yesterday, but the poor woman had been too distraught to take any of it in. 'The last thing she said was to ask if the baby was all right, and then she smiled. She lost consciousness immediately. She's not dead, Doreen; you do understand that, don't you?'

'So she didn't feel any pain?'

'No,' Emma said vehemently. That was one thing she could assure the mother. 'And she's not in pain now.'

'But I don't understand why it

happened,' Doreen said, bewildered. 'Was it because I didn't make her see a doctor sooner?'

'No.' Emma reached out and touched her arm. 'You are in no way to blame. I'm afraid we're not sure yet what happened, but she's in good hands and she's having the best of care.'

She took one last look at the struggling baby, who still had so many mountains to climb, then left the NICU and saw Nick heading towards her. He was unshaven and still wearing the same shirt he'd worn yesterday. His eyes looked pale and bleak against the darkness of the stubble on his face.

'No change,' he answered the question that Emma had not yet put to him. 'I'm going to stick around up there with him for a while, just until Mark's seen him, then I'm going home to get some rest and get cleaned up. I've arranged for Tom O'Donnell to cover for me.'

Emma wanted to apologise for so many things. For not recognising the signs that John was having a TIA prior to the stroke, for letting things go so badly wrong during what should have been a routine operation, for even thinking that this was in some way John's fault.

'They say he's probably been having TIAs for some time. How could I miss this, Emma?'

'We all . . . '

'I knew something was wrong with him.' He was talking to himself now, frowning deeply, trying to figure out where he'd gone wrong. 'Why the hell didn't I insist he see a doctor? And yesterday he asked if I wanted to take Melanie's case and I turned him down.' He looked at Emma as if she might be able to give him an answer, but she could only look back at him with helpless sympathy.

He ran his hand back through his hair and shook his head, then turned and walked away. Emma wanted to run after him and hold him, offer him comfort, but she stood rooted to the spot unable to move, barely able to breathe.

*   *   *

On Saturday morning Rose was walking to the farm shop at the edge of the village and Keira wanted to go with her to see the chickens, which were allowed to run free about the place.

'Go ahead,' Emma said, guiltily relieved to have the opportunity of a little time on her own to gather her thoughts. 'I'm going to head over to the church in a while.'

When they'd gone she went outside and gathered some flowers, then stepped across the road. She'd popped in to see Paige and Melanie yesterday and while there was no change in Melanie's condition, her little girl was doing remarkably well. They'd done a head ultrasound checking for bleeding on the brain and found none. Her grandmother had hardly left the baby's side and would probably remain there for the next three months or so. But it didn't alter the fact that Melanie should have been there, sitting beside her daughter and not lying in an intensive care bed.

Emma knelt down on the grass and emptied the vase, washing it out and refreshing the water before arranging the fresh flowers. For this visit she was silent. She would never let her visits to Daisy's grave become opportunities for her to offload her own unhappiness. And if she couldn't think of anything happy to say, then she didn't speak at all.

'He blames himself, you know,' Nick's voice chased through the stillness. 'He thinks he did something wrong; made a mistake and caused Melanie to crash.'

Emma got to her feet, gathered up the dead flowers and stood before him, feeling helpless. 'It wasn't his fault,' she murmured.

'Damn right it wasn't! The man was ill. And even if he wasn't, there was nothing he could have done to stop what happened. It's a miracle Melanie survived at all. There's something wrong with her heart. The cardiac team are on to it now and hopeful they can put it right. She was born with it and it was a time-bomb ticking away inside her.'

Emma took a step back. 'I should have realised sooner that something was wrong with your father and acted upon it,' she said. 'It wouldn't have helped Melanie, but at least the poor man wouldn't be blaming himself for something that wasn't his fault.'

'Why? Why should you have seen it and not me? His health had been a concern to me for some time, but I chose to ignore it, believing him when he said he was okay, choosing to take the easy option.'

'No,' she said.

'He thinks he was to blame, and you were with him right after. Did you say something to him to give him that idea?'

How could he think that? 'I didn't say anything, but he must have been aware on some level of what was happening in the room.'

Nick seemed not to hear her. He continued, 'Oh, yes. Once you start talking blame, Emma, you have to dish it out to everyone. And the guilt too. Oh, let's not forget the guilt . . . ' He broke off and looked past her at the flowers and a cloud crossed his eyes.

Before she could get in his way, divert him, stop him, he'd brushed past her and was hunkering down at the graveside. She watched, frozen, as he saw the much newer vase in the centre. Her heart contracted as his fingers brushed aside the flowers so that he could read the inscription.

'Daisy?' his voice was a ragged whisper. 'This is the Daisy you . . . ' He couldn't continue. He'd read her date of birth, her date of death and before Emma could utter a word he'd done his sums and had turned to look at her.

'Our Daisy?' he said, his voice like torn paper, harsh and broken. 'Our baby?'

She closed her eyes and nodded. He turned back to look at the grave and stayed where he was, his shoulders rigid, but she knew he was crying. This had been the week from hell and for him the agony just kept piling on.

'There was so much wrong with her,' Emma whispered, her heart aching for him. She wanted to reach out and touch him, but she was afraid that he would push her away. 'A valve in her heart was open and didn't respond to medication, but she was too weak for an operation. And then there were the bleeds in her brain and the pulmonary haemorrhage. They'd no sooner start to get on top of one thing than something else would happen.'

'And what the hell is this supposed to be?' he reached out and tore down the chain of now-dead daisies Keira had draped around the old headstone, crushing the lifeless little flowers in his fists and hurling them to the ground. He stood suddenly and turned round to face her, his face a darkened mask of fury. 'And you kept all this to yourself?' he hissed. 'You didn't even give me a chance to see her? Hold her? My own baby.'

'I didn't want to keep it from you,' she pleaded. 'I tried to contact you.'

'Yes, yes, so you said,' he said. 'And why should I believe that? I would have been there for you, for both of you. You knew where to find me, Emma.'

'No, I didn't,' she said, sobs rising in her throat. She couldn't bear to look at him, to see the naked anger on his face. 'I thought you'd gone.'

'Don't lie,' he said icily. 'We both know I tried to get in touch with you and you chose to ignore me, to shut me out. But how you could keep something like this from me?' He shook his head, then walked past her, leaving a blast of cold air in his wake.

There's more, Emma wanted to tell him. *You only know half the story*. But she couldn't speak. She stayed where she was, rooted to the spot until she heard the roar of his car engine fading into the distance.

And not two minutes later, Rose and

Keira walked in through the church gate, Keira bouncing along merrily hanging on to Rose's hand. Nick must have passed them.

'Are you all right?' Rose asked and Emma composed herself, drew in her breath and brushed dry grass from her knees. Quickly she gathered up the scattered remains of the daisy chain and hid it amongst the other dead flowers.

'Fine,' she said with false cheer. 'Did you see the hens, Keira?'

* * *

As Nick sped down the main street of the village he passed a woman with a child and slowed down. Driving like a maniac wasn't going to change anything. The woman looked like Emma's aunt Rose and the child bouncing along beside her holding her hand looked about five years old. Other than that, blinded by a mixture of grief and rage, he didn't notice anything.

How could she? How could she have

a child and deliberately exclude him? She must have despised him to shut him out like that. Was Daisy what she wanted to talk to him about? It had to be. She said he'd change his mind about her when he knew the truth. Damn right! At least now he saw her for the . . . the what? Dear God, she'd lost a baby. He slowed right down and pulled in at the side of the road. She must have gone through hell during the few short days of Daisy's life, and she'd gone through it alone.

He went over the things she had listed, things that were wrong with the baby, things that couldn't be fixed. Poor little scrap. She hadn't had much of a chance. How had Emma felt to have had to stand by and watch her baby die a little more every day?

What was he thinking to rage at her like that? It explained so much. The time off work, the gradual return to part-time hours. The whole thing must have been so painful for her. And of course, the Daisy at the hospital had brought it all back to her and her grief had been so raw, so real.

But no matter how sorry he felt for her, it didn't alter the fact that she'd deliberately shut him out not just of her life, but also out of their child's life, short as it was. He considered going back to the village, but he was afraid his temper would get the better of him again. Temper, or pain? The two things were very closely linked. Pain, he decided. He wasn't angry, not really, but something was hurting like hell and he only knew it was all Emma's doing.

He returned to the hospital and went straight to see his father. He was making amazing progress, physically at least, but he was being haunted by what had happened to Melanie. His face lit a little when Nick walked in.

'How are you feeling, Dad?'

John Logan sighed. He could speak, but his words were slurred and he seemed to prefer not to say anything at all, not in front of anyone at any rate. The nurses said they had heard him talking to himself, practising his words, struggling to enunciate. He'd already seen a speech therapist who was pretty hopeful of a full recovery of his verbal skills.

All in all he was a lucky man to be in this modern stroke unit and to have come here so quickly and received the crucial immediate treatment. But John Logan looked as if he may well consider himself the most unlucky man on the planet; certainly one of the most unhappy.

'You were asleep when I came in earlier,' Nick said. 'Would you like a drink?'

John nodded and Nick poured him a glass of water from the jug, then held it to his lips. At first John had ignored his right-hand side, but now he was trying to use his right hand, lifting it towards the glass with the help of his own left hand. Always fighting.

Nick helped him to hold the glass and guided it to his lips. A little of the water trickled down his chin and Nick quickly wiped it away with a tissue.

'They're operating on Melanie this

morning.' Nick spoke quietly and John's eyes turned to look at him, his brows lowering. 'There was a fault in her heart, Dad, and there was no way anyone could have known. They're hopeful she'll make a full recovery. You hadn't done anything wrong and there was nothing you or anyone else could have done to change what happened.'

John leaned back against his pillows and closed his eyes. His face still drooped to one side and a tear ran down his cheek. When he opened his eyes again they were red, and he groped for Nick's arm with his right hand and eventually managed to grip hold of it. Once he had his grip sure, he clung on as if his life depended on it.

'Makes no difference.' He forced out the words and it sounded so painful, so difficult. 'Emma . . . ' He couldn't say any more but slumped back, the effort of talking exhausting him.

Damn him! Damn her! What had she said to him?

'Emma was upset,' Nick said, though

why he was making excuses for her, he didn't know.

'Right to be,' John said and closed his eyes again. Nick spoke to him again, but he kept his eyes closed and his grip on Nick's arm slackened. The subject for now was closed.

★ ★ ★

On Monday Emma arrived early at the hospital. She went first to the stroke unit, where she was amazed to find John sitting up in bed eating his breakfast. He was moving his right hand with his left, determined to get his right side mobile again.

'Is it all right if I just pop in and see him?' she asked the ward sister.

'Yes, of course. He's doing very well. He's a very determined man, and he does everything and more the physios ask of him.'

Emma approached the bed slowly. She'd brought some flowers from her garden and held them out in front of her like a shield. The last thing she wanted was to upset him, and she watched his face closely for his reaction. When it came, it was a delighted smile which lifted one half of his face.

She couldn't think what on earth she might have said or done that would make him think she blamed him for Melanie's collapse. It was true that the thought had crossed her mind, but she'd never voiced that thought.

'Emma. Lovely! Flowers. For me?'

'Yes, from my garden.' She smiled, relief flooding through her.

'Pretty.' He smiled and touched the petals. 'I like flowers.'

One of the cleaners smiled and said, 'I'll put those in water for you,' and whisked the flowers away.

'They tell me you're doing very well,' Emma said. 'But how are you feeling, really?'

'Guilty,' he said.

'You have no need to feel guilty. What makes you think you should?'

He frowned. 'I don't remember,' he

said. 'Not the section. I only know Melanie almost died because . . . Nick told me it wasn't my fault; that it was her heart. Should I have known?' His frown deepened and pain filled his eyes. 'How can I not remember?'

'You delivered the baby and she's doing very well,' Emma said, keen to give him some good news. 'You saved the baby, John.'

His troubled face softened. 'Such a shame,' he said, shaking his head sadly. 'Melanie.'

'If it wasn't for you bringing her in when you did, they would have both died,' Emma said, and realised that John was no longer looking at her. She turned and saw Nick approaching.

'What are you doing here?' he said. 'My father is not to be upset.'

'I wasn't . . . '

The protest died on Emma's lips as the cleaner returned and put the flowers on the locker beside John's bed. She flicked the petals with her fingers and smiled. 'They're lovely,' she said, then she smiled even more broadly at John. 'You don't remember me, do you? You're the doctor who delivered my twins. They're both at university now.'

John gave her a bemused smile. 'I remember,' he said, and her eyes filled with tears. And just as Emma was thinking that it was impossible, John added, 'Girls.'

'Yes, Catherine and Emily,' she laughed incredulously. 'Well, fancy you remembering us.'

'I never forget,' John said and the woman walked away, head held high and as pleased as punch.

Nick looked at the flowers, the same kind that Emma had put on their daughter's grave, and his eyes creased with pain. 'I don't want you coming here,' he said coldly.

Emma bit back a sharp reply and leaned over to kiss John's cool cheek. 'Goodbye, John,' she said, squeezing his hand as she spoke. 'Take care.'

'Come back and see me again,' John said, and she smiled as she walked away. 'Ignore him. He doesn't know what he's on about,' John called after her, and she was warmed to hear the humour back in his voice.

Her daughter's grandfather. Now that it no longer mattered what Nick thought of her, since he'd already decided to hate her, the truth could come out. And she would bring Keira to meet John. The smile on her face began to waver as she exited the ward, and by the time she was on the stairs tears were running down her face.

Who was she kidding, that it didn't matter what Nick thought of her? Of course it mattered.

Downstairs she brushed away her tears just as Jimmy came round the corner. 'Ah, the very girl,' he said cheerfully, then he looked more closely. 'Tears? Have you just been to see John? Is he worse?'

'No, he's improving,' she said quickly. 'I just, I . . . '

'Still upset about Melanie, eh?' he said, draping his arm around her shoulders and giving her a squeeze. 'I think that's something that will affect us all for some time. As you're early, what do you say to a nice cup of coffee in the café?'

Why not? She nodded.

'Seen anything of Nick?' Jimmy asked as he carried two cups over to an outside table.

'Just now,' Emma said. She didn't want to think about Nick's anger, the hurt in his eyes, or of what she and he had lost.

'He's not a happy bunny,' Jimmy said. He opened four tubes of sugar and spilled them into his cup.

'So much sugar,' Emma gasped.

'I know,' he grinned. 'You'd think I was sweet enough already. Anyway, we weren't talking about my sweetness, but about Nick. He blames himself for all this, you know.'

'Nick does?'

'He thinks he should have seen the warning signs in his father and Melanie.'

'He told you this?'

'Hell, no!' Jimmy said. 'Nick doesn't share those kinds of feelings with anyone, but I know the guy. He's deep. He broods. He's in love with you as well, which doesn't help matters.'

'Hey, now, that's not true.' Emma sat back in her chair.

'Hey now nothing,' Jimmy said. 'I told you, I know him. I've never seen him this wound up about a woman in the three years I've been working with him. And it's not just work; we're friends, too, you may have gathered.'

'Well . . . ' Emma sighed sadly. 'It may have been true, but not anymore.'

'Oh, why not?'

'He has his reasons,' she said.

'But you love him, right?'

'It isn't as simple as that, Jimmy,' she said and got to her feet. 'Thanks for the coffee. I'll see you around.'

'Indeed you will,' Jimmy said, grinning. '*Au revoir.*'

★ ★ ★

Emma walked into a quiet Monday. Seven babies had been born over the weekend and all but two had been discharged already. Two of the weekend births turned out to be mothers they'd booked in for induction on Monday, both going into labour under their own steam.

As always, once she'd done the hand-over, Emma's first visit was to Jenny. 'Did you have a good weekend?' Emma asked.

'Sure,' Jenny said dryly. 'I went to the theatre and had a meal at a fancy restaurant, then we drove to the beach and I ran barefoot along the sand.'

'Point taken,' Emma said with a grin. 'But you'll be doing those things again soon.'

'I don't know as I will,' Jenny laughed. 'I never did them before I was holed up in here. The theatre bores me, and knowing my luck if I tried running barefoot on the sand I'd find the only piece of broken glass on the beach.'

'But you'll eat out at restaurants,' Emma said.

'Yeah, right, like I'm going to be welcome anywhere with two kids in tow.' She realised what she'd said and covered her mouth. 'Oh, God, I didn't mean it to sound like that. I didn't mean I don't want them.'

'I know you didn't,' Emma said. She was checking the readout on the monitor and had noticed a very slight decrease in the heart rate of one of the twins. It could be nothing to worry about; on the other hand, it could be the start of something.

'We'll be giving you your scan today instead of tomorrow,' Emma said casually.

'Why?'

'It's really quiet here today, so we may as well get a few routine things out of the way,' Emma said with a wry smile. 'Of course if you'd rather wait until tomorrow, we can.'

'No, I don't mind. Anything to break the monotony.'

Emma had hoped she'd say that. She didn't want to do or say anything to alarm Jenny. 'I expect Nick will want to be in on this,' Emma said. 'Particularly as he missed the last one. I'll be back in a while.'

'Don't rush off,' Jenny said. 'I've got something to show you. I haven't just spent the weekend sitting here on my backside feeling sorry for myself.' She reached into her locker and pulled out her knitting needles to which was attacked a slightly wonky knitted square. 'What do you think of that?' she said proudly. 'All my own work. There's a bit of a hole where I dropped a stitch and I seem to have more stitches on the needle than I started with, but what the hey? You were right — it does pass the time.'

*   *   *

Nick sat behind his desk running a pen through his fingers, staring at it but not seeing it. All he could see was Emma. Eyes open or closed, she was there: small, vulnerable, sad. Why had he

239

taken everything out on her — his anger, his hurt? And how could he have condemned her for not getting in touch with him? She thought he was keen to go and live on the other side of the world and when she found herself pregnant, she must have been torn in two worrying about it.

But she'd insisted that he hadn't tried to contact her. Why was that? Why would she lie when she knew perfectly well that he was telling the truth? Unless she really didn't know. What if Rose had never passed his messages on?

He almost didn't hear the soft tap on the door, but heard himself answer, 'Come in.'

He looked up and it was her. She took his breath away. He wanted to hate her, or better still feel nothing for her, but somehow his feelings just seemed more intense than ever. They had lost a child together, the only anomaly being that their grief was separated by almost five years.

'What is it, Emma?'

240

'Jenny,' she said and he dropped the pen and sat upright. 'It may be nothing, but I think we should reschedule her scan.'

'Good idea,' Nick said, reading her mind and doing it correctly as usual. 'Have you said anything to her?'

'I don't want to alarm her unnecessarily.'

'Good,' he said, nodding. 'Quite right. Well there's no time like the present, so set it up and I'll join you in a moment. I'm going to ring her husband.' He checked his watch. 'He'll be at work.'

'Perhaps we should wait,' Emma suggested. 'He says he can be here inside twenty minutes if he has to.'

'Yes, you're right. No need to alarm either of them at this stage. Okay, Emma.' He got up and strode to the door and heard her intake of breath. She smelled wonderful, clean and fresh. But he wasn't about to try and kiss her. Things had progressed beyond that now. Maybe too far beyond that.

'After you,' he said, holding the door open.

She gathered herself and walked past him, careful not to even brush against him as she went by so close. He looked down at the top of her head as she passed. Hell, he liked her hair like that!

★ ★ ★

Emma swirled gel from a tube on Jenny's stomach, then began the scan. Nick had been joking with Jenny from the word go and she hadn't a clue that they were becoming concerned.

'Well,' Nick said with a grin, 'how would you like to be holding your babies sooner rather than later?'

'They're in trouble?' Jenny was instantly alert.

'No, they're not,' he said calmly. 'But one of the babies has a slightly abnormal heartbeat. This is just the sort of thing we have been monitoring you so closely for, Jenny, so that we can intervene before it becomes a problem.'

Jenny drew in her breath and let it out slowly. 'Okay,' she said. 'Okay, do what you have to do. It's funny, but ever since I came in here I've dreaded this moment; and now it's here, I feel pretty damn calm. How about that?'

And that was in no small part due to Nick's attitude. How different it had been at her own scan, Emma thought. The anxiety for her twins had been obvious from the start.

'It'll be the knitting,' Nick laughed.

'That's what it is,' Jenny laughed back and Emma felt the tiniest twinge of envy. There had been nothing like this at the hospital where her twins were born. Perhaps if there had . . . But that was a destructive road to travel. It wouldn't have made any difference if she'd had all the clowns in the world tumbling around in the operating room and was laughing her head off. The outcome would have been the same.

'Hell,' she muttered, 'I don't even like clowns.' She looked up and saw that Jenny and Nick were both staring at her, puzzled looks on their faces. 'Sorry,' she said, flushing with embarrassment. 'Private thoughts.'

'What we have to do is an immediate C-section,' Nick said, taking another look at the screen. 'Would you like us to call your husband?'

'Yes, he'll want to be here,' Jenny said.

'Good, I'll go and do that. Emma, can you get the team together, please?'

He got up from the stool and left the room, whistling as if he hadn't a care in the world. Only Emma knew how concerned he was. This would be a very difficult delivery. But Nick's attitude was that it was all in a day's work and nothing out of the ordinary.

'Just think,' Emma said, 'you could be home in a few days.' She knew that that was what Jenny longed for, only second to having two healthy babies, getting out of this place and going home.

'With my babies?'

'That I can't say.' Emma smiled.

'They're still a little early so may need special care for a while, but I don't think it will be long. They're both a good size and we allow babies smaller than them to go home.' She wiped the gel from Jenny's stomach and covered her up. 'One thing, Jenny. Don't be alarmed by the number of people in the OR. There'll be a neonatal team for each baby plus the surgical team for you. It can seem a little crowded, but everyone has a job to do and I don't want you to feel alarmed or overwhelmed by it all.'

'But you'll be there?'

'Hell, yes,' Emma said. 'I wouldn't miss this for the world.'

Jenny caught her bottom lip with her teeth. 'All those people,' she said resolutely. 'Just for me and my babies.'

'Remember that, Jenny,' Emma said brightly. 'They're all there for you. You may never have this much attention again in your life.'

Jenny gave a dry little laugh. 'Suits me,' she said.

9

Less than an hour after Jenny's scan, Nick was making his incision while Emma watched. He reached in and water gushed over his glove. 'Come on there, little fella,' he murmured as his skilled fingers worked to free the first baby. 'Come say hi to everybody. We're all waiting for you.'

Within seconds he was pulling the first baby through the incision, taking a split second to look him over before handing him to Jimmy. Emma's heart was in her mouth as the baby began to bawl. She laughed. She couldn't help herself. 'It's a little boy,' she told Jenny

'That means the other one will be a boy, right?' Jenny's husband Scott said.

'Right,' Emma said. 'Monoamniotic twins are always the same sex.'

Jimmy hurried round to Jenny's head and bent down so she could see. 'Say hi to Mummy,' he said and the baby bawled his head off, demonstrating that his lungs were perfectly okay thank you very much!

'He's beautiful,' Jenny sobbed. 'Isn't he beautiful, Scottie?'

Her husband was too choked to speak and could only nod.

'I'm just going to take him and check him out,' Jimmy said, then he returned to his team. Wendy Hibbard was waiting for the second baby, the one that was causing all the worry. Emma was watching Nick. The first twin was fine, but this was the crucial moment. The second twin had the cord wrapped round his neck several times and more of it round his body. Nick had to work fast, but at the same time he had to be careful not to cinch the cord.

'He's still crying,' Jenny said, choking on her tears. 'Isn't that a wonderful sound, honey?'

'The best sound in the world,' Scott agreed.

'Emma,' Nick said, and there was

nothing in his voice to give away the tension he felt. Emma moved forward and helped untangle the cord, slowly and carefully. The baby's life depended on the greatest of care at this stage.

The baby had his eyes squeezed shut, but suddenly they opened and squinted at Emma. She almost laughed out loud. Daisy had rarely opened her eyes.

'Here we go,' Nick said and he pulled the baby free, handing him over to Wendy, who was waiting. 'Jenny, you'll have to wait a moment to see this baby. We just have to check him out first.'

'Why isn't he crying?' Jenny strained, trying to lift her head.

'He's fine, honestly,' Emma said. 'I saw him and he's fine. He's just having a little trouble breathing, but that's something we can help him with, okay?'

'I want to hold them,' Jenny cried and her euphoria had turned suddenly to despair. Emma knew how she felt — the desperate need to hold her babies, to make contact.

'Jimmy?' Nick called. Jimmy looked

across and nodded, and moments later came over with the first baby. He put him down on Jenny's chest while Nick finished delivering the placenta, before going on to close the incision. The whole thing from start to finish had taken less than sixty minutes, yet it had felt like a lifetime.

'Four and a half pounds,' Jimmy said. 'How about that, Mummy?'

Jenny began to laugh and cry all at once. Scott reached out and gently stroked the baby's head with his finger.

'Hey, that's not at all bad, munchkin,' Scott said.

Not bad. It was a go-home weight, but Emma knew that they'd want to keep both babies in the NICU for at least one night.

'What's his name?' Emma asked.

'James,' Scott said.

'Good choice.' Jimmy grinned. 'And the other one?'

'Edward,' Jenny said. 'Is he okay? We're not hearing anything.'

'He's not as okay as this little guy, but he's going to be all right,' Nick answered. 'We're going to put him on a ventilator, but I'm sure that's just going to be a temporary situation until he gets to grips with his breathing. He's a whisker under four and a half pounds, by the way; in fact he'd probably have made the same weight as James if he hadn't emptied his bowels as soon as he was born. That's taking identical to the limit,' he laughed.

While the twins were taken to the NICU, Emma settled Jenny back in a quiet side room. She washed her and helped her into a clean nightdress while Scott went up to the NICU to see how the babies were getting on.

'You're going to feel tired for a few days,' Emma warned her. 'And you may experience some after-pain, but if you do, let us know and we can give you pain relief. There's no need for you to be uncomfortable.'

'I just want to see my babies,' Jenny said. She'd said it a dozen times since leaving the OR.

'You will, but not until tomorrow.'

Emma smiled. 'Scott's with them now and I promise you, they won't be alone.'

'How did you know?' Jenny asked.

'What's that?'

'How did you know that I'd be worrying about them being alone?'

Because I've been in your shoes, Emma thought, and she wished with all her heart she could tell Jenny just how similar their experiences were. But she couldn't. It wouldn't do Jenny any good at all right now to hear that Emma had lost one of her babies, even though neither James nor Edward were in any immediate danger.

When the door opened, Jenny looked up expectantly, but it was Nick. 'I've just been to see your twins,' he said with a broad grin. 'They're both doing very well. Edward is on a ventilator, but I think Jimmy explained to you that it won't be for long. They'll stay in the NICU until tomorrow at least, but I'll check you out tomorrow and if I think you're fit, I'll take you up there to see them myself.'

'In a wheelchair,' Emma put in.

'Well I wasn't going to make her walk,' Nick laughed.

'I just want to thank you both,' Jenny said tearfully. 'Everyone's been great here, but you delivered my babies safely, Nick. And you — ' She turned to Emma and reached for her hand. ' — you seemed to understand how I felt more than anyone else I spoke to. It's almost as if you've been through the same thing yourself.'

'Bless you,' Emma said, aware that Nick was staring at her.

Soon afterwards, Scott returned and Emma and Nick left them on their own. Scott had been taking photographs and Jenny was keen to view them on the camera's little screen.

*　*　*

'Come for a coffee, Emma? It's time for a break,' Nick said as they left the room.

'Oh, I have a lot to do.'

'Go on,' he said and something about

252

his voice made her agree.

'Okay,' she said, but she didn't know why. Perhaps he was going to tell her again to keep away from his father.

They walked to the café without speaking and when they got there, Nick told her to wait outside. He came out a few moments later with two coffees to take away.

'I thought we could go and sit outside by the lake,' he said. 'It's quieter out there, if that's okay with you.'

She nodded. They didn't sit on the benches provided, but on the low brick wall surrounding one of the raised flower beds. Emma cupped her hands around the mug and sipped her coffee slowly.

'I'm sorry, Emma,' Nick said. He was gripping his own cup, staring into the white froth on the top.

'Sorry?'

'For everything.' He looked up and narrowed his eyes as if it hurt too much to have them wide open. 'For letting you down five years ago. For accusing you of blaming Dad. I don't know why I did that. He was confused, he said some things that I took the wrong way, and I ended up adding two and two together and getting fifteen!'

'That bad, huh?' Emma laughed softly.

'Oh, yes,' he said, laughing gently himself.

'I'm sorry too,' she said, licking her lips and then biting them. 'I'm sorry that I didn't believe enough in you and that I was willing to think you'd just go and carry on your life as if nothing had happened. And I'm sorry that my aunt didn't pass on your messages.'

'She didn't?'

Emma shook her head. 'Don't be mad at her, Nick. She's so cut up about it.'

'She is?' She could see anger was rising within him, ready to explode. He was still teetering on the brink of his ragged emotions.

'Yes, Nick, she is,' Emma said calmly.

'At first she thought if I came back to you that we'd go to Australia together. I'm all she has, Nick. Well, me and Keira.'

'Huh?'

It was impossible not to mention her daughter. Keira was too big a part of her life. 'Rose saved me when I was a child, Nick. If it hadn't been for her I would have ended up in care, and while I know damn well it isn't hell for everyone, my life could have ended up a whole lot differently to how it has.'

He upended his mug, tipping the contents onto the bark on the raised flower bed.

'Who is Keira?' He crushed the empty mug in his fist and hurled it into a bin. 'Who,' he repeated stonily, 'is Keira?'

There was no putting this off any longer. Emma had dropped herself right in this mess and now she had to dig herself out of it. This wasn't how she'd meant to tell him about their daughter.

'Daisy was a twin,' she stammered and while she was scared, it felt like such a relief to finally, finally have the truth out in the open. She wouldn't have to bite her tongue every time she began to mention Keira's name. 'Keira is her sister.'

'Is?'

'They were monoamniotic twins, like Jenny's,' Emma explained and Nick sprang to his feet and turned his back to her. She could see he was clenching and unclenching his fists. Was he mad? Happy? Upset? Without being able to see his face, she couldn't tell. When he finally turned to look at her, she still couldn't tell. His face was a mask, betraying nothing of what he felt.

'I have a little girl,' he said, and the only hint to what he was feeling was the note of wonder in his voice.

'Yes.' Emma smiled nervously. 'You do. And she's beautiful.'

'I'm a father,' he said, still in awe. 'I never thought . . . a father.'

'I'm sorry I didn't tell you before, Nick, but . . . '

He wasn't listening. He was deep in

thought, but his eyes were bright. 'That makes Dad a grandfather,' he said at last. 'After all this time, he'd given up hope. Emma, I've watched that man practise everything from his speech to his movement, but the one thing I long to see is his smile, however lopsided it might be. And I don't mean the polite smile he gives when you go to visit; I mean the real deal, the one that illuminates his whole face.'

Emma felt a little stung. Heck, she felt very stung. She'd just told him they had a child and all he could think of was the effect the news would have on his father!

'I want to meet her,' he said, something vital shining in his eyes as he looked at her.

'I won't let you use her, Nick,' Emma said with some suspicion. 'I won't let you dangle her like a carrot under your father's nose until she's served her purpose. I won't let you just drop her if something better comes along. She's a human being. She's a bright and funny little person, mature beyond her years, and yet as bonny as any other child her age.' She found herself smiling as she described the daughter she adored. 'She knows you exist, Nick. I've always told her that she'd meet you one day, but it's only something I'll allow to happen under the right circumstances.'

He looked taken aback. 'You don't want us to meet?'

'I didn't say that.'

'Then what the hell are you saying, Emma? Make up your mind. You think I'd walk into her life and then walk straight back out of it again so easily? You think . . . oh, God.' He broke off and put his hand to his head. 'The daisy chain,' he whispered. 'That was Keira's, wasn't it? And I destroyed it. I wish you'd told me before, Emma, I really do. I wish . . . ' He took his hand from his head and held it out in a gesture of pure helplessness. What was the point in wishing anything?

'Can I tell my father about Keira?' Nick asked. 'I wouldn't normally rush you into a decision like this, but I'd hate it if he . . . if he never got to hear that he was a grandfather.'

'We could tell him together,' Emma suggested. She understood what Nick was saying. He was afraid he might lose his father before he could be given the news. It wasn't likely now, especially given the speed of his improvement, but it must be at the back of Nick's mind how close he'd come to losing him already.

'Now?' he asked.

'Why not?'

It was all out in the open now, but still Emma didn't feel right. Nick's reaction hadn't been quite what she expected, but when she thought about it, she had no idea what she'd expected anyway. Happily ever after, maybe. Perhaps this had brought it home to him that any relationship with Emma would include a child. Perhaps he didn't want that kind of responsibility — or perhaps he wanted it too much.

Nick had never felt like this before

— as if everything inside him was churning and tumbling like clothes being tossed about in a washing machine.

A daughter. A living, breathing daughter. What did she look like? He should have asked. But he couldn't ask now, because they were hurrying into the stroke unit. And then he remembered the woman he saw in the village — the woman he thought might be Rose, and the bouncing, happy child holding her hand.

Was that Keira? His daughter? The thought flooded him with warmth. He wished he'd taken more notice of her. He kept looking at Emma and felt nothing but awe and wonder. The birth of a baby never failed to move him deeply, but the thought that she had given birth to his daughters — well, it just blew him away. And he didn't know how to tell her that, and wasn't even sure she'd want to hear it. After all, she'd gone through the worst and the best of it alone. He felt a little like some kind of Johnny-come-lately, hoping to have some part in his daughter's life.

His daughter. God, that sounded good. *Their* daughter sounded even better.

John Logan was in a wheelchair in the balcony room, which looked out over the hospital grounds. His chair was pushed up against a table and he was playing a game of chess with another patient.

Emma and Nick stood watching for a while, both of them admiring the effort he made to move the pieces with his right hand — always helped along by his left hand, which must ache by now surely from doing twice the work. The almost dead weight of a hand and an arm was no light thing to haul about.

His opponent moved his bishop, who now had a clear run at the king. John stared at the board for what seemed an age, then moved his remaining knight into position, blocking the bishop's path to the king.

'Drat,' his opponent swore. John

chuckled softly and moved his queen so that nothing now could save his opponent's king.

'Checkmate,' he said.

'Never play chess with my father,' Nick whispered. 'He can't be beaten.'

They walked over to the table and Nick smiled at the other man, who was carefully replacing the chess pieces in a box. 'Do you mind if we take him away?' he asked, taking hold of the handles of his father's wheelchair.

'No, I don't,' the man huffed. 'Take him away, please, take him away, and don't bring him back. I don't know how he does it.'

Nick wheeled him over to a quiet corner near the window, then he and Emma sat down facing John.

'What is this?' John said slowly. 'It looks like a delegation.'

'We've something to tell you, Dad,' Nick said.

'Something nice?'

'I think so,' Nick said, grinning. 'I think you'll think so too.'

'You're getting married,' John said, and there was the smile Nick so longed to see.

'No, we're not,' Nick said. *Not yet, anyway,* he added silently to himself, *but I'm still working on that one.* 'Emma, would you like to tell him?'

She looked confused, as if she didn't know what to say. Did he really just say what she thought he did? Nick nodded his encouragement and she drew in her breath.

'How do you feel about being a grandfather?' she blurted out, and John laughed his slightly lop-sided laugh, then he stopped abruptly and studied their faces, each one in turn.

'You're not joking?' he said at last.

'John, when Nick and I split up I didn't realise it, but I was pregnant, expecting monoamniotic twins.'

John blinked and looked puzzled. 'That's Jenny,' he said.

'Yes, the same as Jenny,' Nick agreed.

'I lost one of the babies,' Emma went on. 'Her name was Daisy.'

Nick reached out and held her hand. It must be difficult to talk about Daisy. It hurt him like hell and he'd never even seen her. Emma didn't pull her hand away. Instead she gave him a watery smile and continued. 'I called my . . . our other daughter Keira,' Emma said. 'She's five, she's beautiful, and I'd like you to meet her.'

Nick tore his eyes from Emma and looked at his father. Tears were welling in John's eyes and spilling onto his cheeks.

'Dad, are you all right?'

'Thank you,' John whispered. 'Oh, thank you. I would love to meet her too.'

'Is the weekend soon enough?' Emma asked. 'I want to have time to talk to her about all this first.'

It wasn't soon enough for Nick. He wanted to see her right now, gaze in wonder at the little being that he and Emma had created, but he knew Emma was right. It wouldn't be fair to plunge Keira right into a meeting with two strangers.

'The weekend will be fantastic,' Nick said gratefully.

Emma nodded. She seemed distracted. Worried, probably. She stood up and bent to kiss John's cheek.

'I have to get back,' she said. 'I'll see you at the weekend, John.'

I hope so, Nick thought as he watched her hurry away. He hoped to God she didn't take it into her head to disappear again. Well if she did, he wouldn't give up looking for her a second time, her or their daughter.

★ ★ ★

Rose was delighted when Emma told her that Keira was going to meet Nick and John at the weekend. 'Did you tell Nick that it was me?' she asked. It seemed to be her only concern, what Nick would think of her. She'd always been very fond of him, even if she had conspired to keep them apart.

'Yes, I did,' Emma said. 'And he's not mad at you. It's too late for all that now.

He knows that. He understands why you did what you did.'

'Yes, and he must think me a terribly selfish old woman,' Rose said. 'Which I am.'

'Are not,' Emma argued. 'I've never met anyone less selfish in my life. You made a bad decision at a time when you were under a lot of stress, and it was one of those situations that just grew out of control.'

'I'm so lucky,' Rose breathed. 'So very lucky. I could have ended up losing you over this.'

'Never,' Emma declared. She kissed her aunt's cheek and watched as she walked through to her own back garden, then with one last wave she closed the door. She turned and there was Keira standing right behind her. Keira, who was supposed to be upstairs cleaning her teeth before bedtime.

'Who's Nick?' she asked.

'Well actually, sweetie, I wanted to talk to you about Nick this evening,' she said, taking Keira's hand and leading her through to the sitting room. She sat down in one of the big armchairs and pulled Keira onto her lap. Keira rested her head against Emma's shoulder and sighed. She smelled so wonderful and just felt so good in Emma's arms. She felt she could have sat like that forever.

'Is Nick my daddy?' Keira asked before Emma could say a word. 'Is he the man in the photographs?'

'Yes,' she answered truthfully. 'I told you that your daddy was a doctor, didn't I?'

'Yes, a very clever and very important doctor.' Keira echoed the words her mother had used every time she referred to her father. 'And very handsome, too.'

'Well, yes, he is. He's a doctor at the Bob with me, and he very much wants to meet you.'

'Really?' Keira sat up and clapped her hands together, her joy obvious. 'That would be great, Mummy! It's what I wished on the stars for — to have a daddy.'

'And that's not all,' Emma said, laughing with relief. 'You get a bonus granddad as well.'

Keira's eyes widened, and she had the look of a child who had just been told that Christmas and her birthday were being rolled into one and given to her all at once.

'A granddad?' she whispered at last.

'Yes, darling. But he's been a little bit poorly so he's a patient in the hospital at the moment. But . . . '

Keira wriggled off her lap and began to dance around the room. 'I've got a daddy,' she sang happily. 'I've got a granddad!'

* ★ *

The next morning Emma pushed a very eager Jenny along to the NICU to see her sons properly for the first time. She felt ridiculously excited on Jenny's behalf. She knew exactly how Jenny was feeling, and that made her own emotions teeter on a knife edge.

Jimmy was waiting for them. Emma had already called ahead to make sure this was an appropriate time for a visit. He led them over to Edward, and then stood back and watched as Jenny's face absolutely crumpled.

'Edward, I've brought your mummy along to see you,' Emma murmured.

'Edward,' Jenny's voice cracked. 'But I thought he was on a ventilator?'

'Not anymore,' Jimmy said, grinning. 'Congratulations, Mummy, your second-born has overcome his first big hurdle — he's breathing on his own. His blood pressure is a little low, but we're treating him for that.'

While Jimmy spoke, Jenny reached in through one of the armholes in the side of the incubator.

'Can I touch him?' she asked shakily.

'Of course.'

Emma was almost choked by a lump the size of a football that suddenly seemed to lodge in her throat as Jenny gently stroked her baby's leg.

'Hi Eddie,' Jenny said, tears of joy

coursing down her face. 'Hi, my beautiful little boy.' Then she looked up at Jimmy imploringly. 'Can't I hold him?'

Jimmy hesitated for a split second. Sometimes being held could prove stressful for the babies, but there was no doubt that Edward was responding positively to the sound of his mother's voice.

'There's another little boy wanting your attention,' Jimmy said with a smile. 'Come say hi to James, and then we'll arrange for you to hold both of them.'

Emma turned the wheelchair and heard Jenny's gasp when she saw her other baby. James was looking out of the incubator with slate-blue eyes.

'If all goes well, we're moving them both out of NICU today,' Jimmy said. 'They'll go into the intensive care nursery, which is a step closer to going home — and before you ask, we're looking at keeping them here for a maximum of six weeks, but I've a pretty

270

good idea it'll be closer to two.'

'Wow,' Jenny gasped. 'Hi, James. Did you hear that? Six weeks maximum and then you're coming home. You should see your room.'

The whole thing was so emotionally charged that Emma felt as if she might burst into tears herself at any minute. She'd got to know Jenny so well during her stay in the hospital, and this was the most wonderful outcome they could have hoped for.

'Is Hubby coming in this morning?' Jimmy asked.

'No,' Jenny said. 'He'll be in after lunch. Why?'

'I was going to say it'd be a nice photo opportunity — first time the boys are reunited since leaving the womb.'

'Well Emma could do it,' Jenny said eagerly. 'You could hold one of them, couldn't you?'

'Well, I . . . ' Why was she hesitating? Emma's emotions began to stumble and crash about like waves driven onto a rocky beach. She hadn't held a baby in the NICU since Daisy.

She looked at Jenny's hopeful tear-stained face. Was it really fair to make her wait for this moment?

'I'd be honoured,' Emma said at last.

★   ★   ★

Nick glanced through the window of the NICU and saw Jenny in her wheelchair and Emma sitting in a chair beside her. They were each holding one of Jenny's twins. He could see Emma from the side, her head bowed as she looked down at the baby in her arms.

Slam! His heart rocked against his ribs, blasting his breath out of him. He leant his head against the glass, but couldn't take his eyes off her. There was a small smile on her face and she was talking, but he knew her well enough to know she was barely holding it together.

He didn't know how long he stood there watching before Jimmy stooped and spoke to Emma and one of the neonatal nurses took the baby she was holding out of her arms. She stood up almost as soon as she was relieved of the baby. Stood up and looked around as if she was lost. Jimmy said something to her and she nodded and fled from the NICU out into the corridor, where she looked up and down wildly before turning on her heel and running like hell for the exit.

Jimmy came out behind her, saw Nick and called out, 'Did you see Emma? Something's not right. I'll take Jenny back . . . go!'

Go! His feet had been rooted, but now he was running as well, running for all he was worth just in time to see Emma bursting open the fire doors and running into the hospital grounds, where she broke stride for a moment and looked about in confusion before the doors slowly closed behind her.

'Emma,' he called as he burst out of the fire doors behind her and saw her still running across the grass, getting further and further away from the hospital buildings.

She stopped suddenly and he could see her shoulders heaving up and down as she gulped in lungfuls of air. 'Emma, love! Oh, love.' He put his hands on her shoulders and turned her gently to face him. Her face was awash with tears, her eyes luminous with grief, pain and joy. He knew without her having to say a word that it was a mixture of all three, and probably a lot more besides. He hadn't been there for her when it had really mattered, but he was here now. He wrapped his arms around her and pulled her against him, and he didn't give a damn who saw them or what the hospital grapevine made of all this.

She buried her face in his chest and wept while he stroked her hair and kissed the top of her head, trying desperately to offer comfort. If she were any other grieving mother, he would know all the right things to say, but she wasn't any other; she was Emma.

'I'm sorry,' she managed to stammer out the words at last. 'I don't know what came over me in there. Stupid. Stupid.'

'You're not stupid,' he said, tilting her chin so that he could look at her face — her beautiful, tear-drenched face. 'You're a human being. What you did in there must have been so hard.'

'I'm always holding babies,' she cried. 'It's my job!'

'But not in that setting, under those circumstances,' Nick murmured. 'Come on. Let's get you a coffee or a cup of tea.'

'I don't want tea, Nick,' she ground out the words.

He looked down at her. He'd never felt so helpless in all his life.

'I want . . . I want . . . '

She looked up at him, made a noise like a strangled scream, then turned and stomped off back towards the hospital. Nick watched her go. Did she want him to back off, was that it? My God, why did women have to be so damn complicated? Especially this one!

He looked up and saw the sun

balcony of the stroke unit and a lone figure standing at the window. Standing!

'Dad!'

As he watched, his father turned around and walked away from the window.

Maybe it wasn't him. Maybe it was some other tall man with white hair and a dark red dressing gown. Maybe he was seeing things now on top of everything else.

10

Emma's arms swung indignantly at her sides as she marched back into the hospital. Woe betide anyone who crossed her path today!

As for Nick! What was she to do with him? Just now, out there, she wanted him to kiss her because somehow, a kiss from him would have just made everything normal again. But instead, he offered her tea. Tea, for goodness sake!

She didn't want tea. She wanted him to tell her that everything would be all right, that *they* would be all right.

Back on the ward she looked in on Jenny, who was tucked up in bed asleep after her adventure. Then Emma made herself busy. Busy, busy, busy.

And later she saw Nick stroll in as if nothing had happened. He stopped by the desk to joke with Val, and Val giggled and blushed and he laughed and it was all so normal.

He couldn't be feeling any of this turmoil that raged around inside Emma. Probably didn't feel anything at all, damn him. He moved on to his office and shut himself inside without a word to her or even a smile in her direction.

Well thanks for nothing, she thought angrily. He'd shut her out when he shut that door, made his feelings towards her perfectly clear. *Thanks a bunch, Nick Logan!*

★　★　★

Once inside his office with the door shut, Nick let out his breath in a rush. Well that was easy, he thought. Walking in like nothing had happened. Pretending Emma was just another fixture around here, paying her no more attention than he did to the fire extinguisher on the wall. Easy.

Who was he kidding? So what now?

Saturday he'd meet Keira. They'd bring her here to meet Dad and then spend the day out at the zoo maybe. Emma would want to tag along of course, but he wasn't going to be able to ignore her then. She'd just have to put up with it if he tried to make polite conversation or if he was stupid enough to make the gigantic mistake of offering her tea!

They'd both have to grin and bear it for Keira's sake. And on that subject, he intended to make some kind of substantial contribution to his daughter's upbringing. And if Emma was too proud to accept any kind of payment, then he'd set up a fund for Keira. Something to see her through university, maybe med school.

That gave him a thought. He went to the door and flung it open and she was still standing there where she'd been when he'd came in. 'Emma,' he said and she looked up as if she hadn't heard the door open, hadn't even noticed him go in there just moments ago.

'Yes?' she said, almost distractedly as if he'd interrupted her in the middle of something of vital importance.

'Keira,' he said. 'Does she want to be a doctor?'

That produced a hell of a smile. It melted his insides, shaved inches off his resolve and almost undid him.

'No,' she said at last. 'Keira wants to be a vet.'

'A vet.' He nodded and went back into his office. Vets have to train for years. It was going to have to be quite a substantial fund. He smiled. A vet, eh? Hadn't he toyed with that idea for some time as a kid himself? His father had put him off, telling him he would have to put down animals that were sick. The very thought had made an eight-year-old Nick sick to his stomach. It wasn't an argument he would ever use to put Keira off. But if she wanted to be a vet, she obviously loved animals. His smile widened. The zoo, then, on Saturday. Perfect.

'Yes, for the umpteenth time, I'm sure I don't want to come along,' Rose said when Emma asked yet again if she'd like to spend the day with them. She looked scared, frightened of her first meeting with Nick, but Emma was sure things would be all right. 'And do I look OK?' she asked.

Rose looked her up and down as if she hadn't already done so half a dozen times. Emma was wearing a white top and jeggings and she was worried that she looked too casual, too young even.

'You look great,' Rose said.

'And Keira?'

In the denim dungarees she loved with a white T-shirt, Keira looked absolutely charming. Her blonde curls formed a cloud around her pretty little face and her smoky eyes were glossy with excitement.

At last a car pulled up outside. It wasn't the silver sports car Nick usually drove, but a big black four-by-four, the kind of vehicle parents used to ferry carloads of children around in, and it was brand new.

'John's with him,' Emma cried. 'He must have been discharged. Oh Rose, won't you please come too?'

'No.' Rose shook her head. 'I can't. Nick . . . '

'He'll be fine, I promise,' Emma said.

Rose bit her lip. 'All right, then. I'll just nip to mine and get a light jacket. As long as you're sure Nick won't mind . . . '

Emma didn't care if Nick minded or not. She wanted backup in the form of her aunt. And the more of them there were, the less likely there was to be awkward silences.

Nick came down the path looking more gorgeous than he had any right to be in denim jeans and a leather jacket. And he was carrying flowers.

'Is that him?' Keira joined Emma at the window.

'Yes, darling.'

They went to the door together and

opened it before Nick had chance to knock. His face broke into a smile — that smile, no less; the one that kicked like a mule.

'Hi, Emma,' he said, handing Emma the flowers. 'Hi, Keira.'

When he looked down at Keira he couldn't seem to stop gazing at her, and she was transfixed by him too. Talk about love at first sight, Emma thought as Nick and their daughter traded admiring glances with identical smoky eyes.

The moment was charged with electricity. There was chemistry at work here, strong chemistry. Emma felt almost excluded and curiously the thought didn't displease her. She wanted Nick to love Keira. She wanted Keira to love Nick. Right at this moment her own feelings just didn't come into it. All that mattered were the feelings of the two people she loved most in all the world.

Keira held out her hand and Nick shook it. 'I'm . . . ' he began and Emma was aware that she should be making the introductions, but frankly speech was beyond her at this point. She wasn't sure what she'd expected, but it certainly hadn't been this immediate connection between father and daughter.

Keira was a friendly, outgoing child, but normally reserved with strangers. Not so with Nick. But Emma could see pain in Nick's eyes too. Whatever he might have said before about understanding and being fine with everything, it must have hit him like a sledgehammer when he actually met Keira.

'You like the zoo, Keira?' Nick asked.

'Wow, yes.' Keira began to bounce, then remembered herself and smiled politely instead. 'Yes, thank you.'

'Well thank you,' Nick said, grinning. 'I like the zoo, too, and now I have the best reason in the world to go. It's a long drive though. You don't mind long drives?'

'I love car journeys,' Keira responded and Emma had the feeling that Keira would gladly sit in a car for a week if it meant being with the father she had yearned for so long to meet and seemed to instantly adore.

He held out his hand and she slipped her tiny one into his. Emma watched in stunned disbelief as the pair of them walked towards the car. She'd been so worried about this moment, deep down fearing that they might not like each other. How could she ever have had such thoughts? Look at them! You'd think they'd known each other all Keira's life.

'Hey! Hey,' Emma called, running to catch up. 'I told Aunt Rose she could come too. I hope that's okay.'

Nick's face froze. His eyes turned to ice. Emma could see straight away that it was very much not okay.

'I mean when I saw the size of the . . . bus, I thought there'd be plenty of room. New, is it?'

Nick laughed tightly. 'Brand new. I want something safe and solid to drive my daughter around in. I've got a car seat for Keira too. The safest one I could get with all the bells and whistles.'

Keira grimaced until she saw the seat. 'Wow,' she gasped again. 'It's like a seat in a space rocket!'

'Hello, John,' Emma said as she climbed into the back of the car beside Emma and breathed in the new leather smell of the seats. 'They've discharged you?'

'Into the care of my son,' he said with a rueful smile. 'And with a wheelchair in the boot. Are you going to introduce us?'

'Keira this is . . . '

'Grandpa,' Keira interrupted. 'I know. You're just how I imagined a grandpa would look. Hello, Grandpa, I'm Keira.' She leant over between the front seats and to Emma's utter astonishment Keira kissed John's cheek, which produced a laugh which was nothing short of gleeful from the older man. Then she got into the car seat and sat patiently while Nick adjusted the straps to fit her correctly. She chatted to him the whole time, telling him about school, about her friend Suki and about her teacher.

Emma listened to Keira's bright little-girl voice occasionally broken up by Nick's deeper tones. It was a joy to hear.

'Are you sure you're feeling up to a day out, John?' Emma asked.

'I have my doctor's permission,' John chuckled. 'Especially since I'm being accompanied by a doctor and a nurse.'

'You must promise to tell us if you feel at all unwell,' Emma said.

'Nick's already made me promise that,' John said. 'And I will. I've learned my lesson.'

By the time Nick had finished making sure Keira was secure and comfortable, Rose was fiddling about with the lock on the front door. She hadn't just picked up a jacket; she'd also changed into a smart cream trouser suit and had added a dash of lipstick.

'I'll go and give her a hand,' Nick said.

Emma held her breath as Nick walked back up the path to speak to Rose. What would he say? If he said one word to upset her . . . But she couldn't hear what was being said and both Nick and Rose had their backs to her.

★　★　★

'How could you do it, Rose?' Nick said coldly. 'How could you do it to Emma? She needed me. My children needed me. You had no right to keep us apart.'

'I know,' Rose said, her hand shaking as she tried to fit the key in the lock. 'But Nick, if you knew how sorry I was . . .'

'Sorry? That doesn't even start to cut it, Rose. You lied to us both and if Emma hadn't come to work at the same hospital as me, I would never have known about my daughter. Do you realise how that feels? Do you have any idea of the damage you did?'

Rose let out a long, heavy sigh. 'Yes, I do. It haunts me, Nick. I hate myself sometimes, but once I started telling lies, I couldn't stop. I was so frightened of losing Emma.'

'She was never yours to lose,' he said

harshly. 'And you'd have happily let us go on living in ignorance for the rest of our lives. You would have deprived my little girl of a father. There are no words to describe how that makes me feel about you, Rose. I thought you were a nice person. It seems I was wrong.'

Rose straightened up. 'You're wrong, Nick. I wasn't happy about it at all. Not a day passed that I didn't regret what I did. But you're right about me not being a nice person. I'm a selfish idiot. I don't deserve Emma or Keira.'

'No,' he said. 'You don't.'

'Perhaps it's best if I don't come today,' Rose said shakily and Nick felt a stab of regret. He felt like the worst kind of bully, but there was nothing he could do to calm his anger. He wanted to grab the woman and shake her, make her understand what she'd done, because however sorry she was and however much she said she regretted it, they couldn't turn back time. Those years were lost and he hadn't had the opportunity to hold his other baby, little Daisy.

'Come on, you two!' Emma called from the car. 'The zoo will be closed by the time we get there.'

'It seems you have to come,' Nick said, taking the key out of Rose's trembling fingers and shoving it into the door, twisting it, then thrusting it back at her. 'Just . . . Just keep away from me and my family.'

'Ooh . . . ' Rose stumbled backwards. 'Nick . . . '

'I mean it, Rose. You won't get another chance to ruin our lives. I have every intention of making a new life for Emma and Keira and the way I feel right now, I don't want you in it.'

Nick held the car door open and Rose climbed in. Her cheeks were very flushed and her eyes looked bright, as if she'd been crying.

'Are you all right, Rose?' Emma asked.

'Yes, I'm fine,' Rose replied shakily. 'Couldn't get the silly key to turn in the lock. Nick did it for me.'

'We'll have to get that lock seen to,' Emma said and Rose turned her face away and looked out of the window.

She's upset, Emma thought. *But what about? Nick wouldn't have said anything to upset her, would he?*

'Off we go,' John said from the front seat. 'Off to the zoo!'

This, Emma thought, was going to be one of the weirdest kinds of family day out ever.

When they arrived at the zoo after more than two hours of driving and a great deal of chatting, especially from Keira, Nick lifted his father's wheelchair out of the boot and opened it up, then insisted John sit in it.

'You're not up to trudging up and down round here all day,' he said sternly.

'I've been sitting down for ages,' John said, 'in the car.'

'You can have a walk round later, John,' Emma said. 'You don't want to overdo things right at the start and end up tiring yourself out.'

'All right, you don't have to gang up on me,' John said with a smile, and he sat down in the chair.

Rose hadn't joined in the chatter. In fact she'd been silent for most of the journey, gazing out of the window, miles away. Even now she stood next to the car, chewing on her lip, looking worried.

'You definitely turned everything off,' Emma whispered. 'And Nick locked the front door. Try to enjoy yourself — it's a lovely day.'

Rose smiled, but it didn't go anywhere near her eyes.

John looked up at her and frowned. 'Feeling a bit car-sick?' he asked.

'Yes,' Rose said. 'A little. I'm glad to be out in the fresh air. Actually, I can push,' she went on, taking hold of the handles. 'Go on, let me, Nick. I do this every Sunday. I walk people out from the nursing home when it's nice weather.'

'All right,' Nick said at last. 'If you're sure.'

'I'm sure. I'd like to feel useful.'

'This is only a temporary situation,' John insisted. 'I won't be in this thing forever.'

'Of course you won't,' Rose said

briskly. 'Where shall we go first? Do you fancy finding somewhere we can sit down and have a cup of tea?'

John thought that was hilarious. He burst out laughing. 'I am sitting down,' he said. 'But I know what you mean. I could murder a cup of tea and maybe a doughnut or a pastry. What do you say, Rose?'

'I say it's an excellent idea,' she said.

Nick and Emma stood with Keira between them. They seemed unsure what to do next.

'Well we don't mean you should join us,' John said with a huff. 'Go on, get yourselves off and have some fun time together. We'll be all right.'

Well that tore it, Emma thought a little later when Rose and John disappeared. *So much for safety in numbers.* 'At least she's cheered up a bit,' Emma said. 'She seemed a bit sad in the car. She feels really bad about what happened, Nick.'

'So she should,' he said, staring off into the distance.

'Would you like me to vanish too, Nick?' Emma whispered. 'Perhaps you'd like to spend some time alone with Keira so you can get to know her better.'

He grabbed her hand. 'I want you along too, Emma,' he said fiercely, and she thought maybe he didn't feel quite as comfortable as it appeared with their daughter. But he didn't let go of her hand for a long time, and when he did it was with a reluctant smile.

Nick handed Keira a very expensive-looking digital camera and let her take shots of just about anything that moved. When she wasn't taking photographs she held tightly to Nick and Emma's hands, walking in between them, keeping them close but apart. A few times their eyes met over her head, and once Nick mouthed, 'She's adorable.'

Emma felt a silly twinge of pride then mouthed back, 'She's your daughter too.'

Sometimes Emma found her hand in Nick's and they'd be walking along together, just like any other young couple with a child. Keira took photographs of them. She seemed utterly delighted by it all.

After two hours of walking round, Keira announced she was hungry, so Nick led the way to one of the zoo cafés. 'I'm a vegetarian,' she told Nick earnestly and he smiled and looked at Emma, remembering how she said that she often cooked vegetarian meals.

'Let's all be vegetarians today,' Nick said, to Keira's delight.

'Should we try to find Rose and John?' Emma said worriedly. 'We haven't seen them at all since we arrived.'

'They'll find us when they want to,' Nick said, as unconcerned as Emma was concerned. 'Relax. They're both grown-ups. Dad has his phone with him, and I bet Rose has one too.'

'Doesn't go anywhere without it.' Emma smiled wryly. 'I'm sure it's in case I need her. She's always been there for me, Nick. Always.'

'I know that now,' he said huskily.

'And they're doing this for us,' he continued, his eyes holding hers in a meaningful gaze. 'So we can be alone together.'

'For Keira,' Emma agreed.

'For all of us,' Nick said as if there really was an 'us' to do anything for.

After lunch they found John and Rose sitting in the sunshine. 'Have you eaten?' Emma asked, and she was about to deliver a lecture about the importance of eating regular meals when Rose laughed.

'I told you she'd say that, didn't I?' she said. 'Yes, love, we've eaten. We've also had plenty to drink and managed to find the loos. We're heading for the gift shop next, so I hope you've got plenty of space in that boot of yours, Nick.' She looked at him, her lips trembling as if it was a huge effort to smile.

'I hope so too,' Nick said pleasantly. 'I certainly have no intention of leaving here empty-handed. I think we'd all like something to remember this day by.'

Well I for one will never forget it, Emma thought. It was the day all their lives would change forever. Nothing would be, *could* be the same after today. Keira had a father. He would meet her out of school sometimes, take her on trips and have her spend the day at his house. And he would probably come to visit Daisy with them. There might even be holidays when he would take Keira away for a week or more at a time. Emma didn't want to think about that. And what if Nick got married? Emma would have half-brothers and sisters and a step-mother. That was something she definitely did not want to think about.

★   ★   ★

They arrived home in the late afternoon. They would have stayed at the zoo until it closed, but John was showing signs of fatigue and none of them wanted him to overdo it. He slept for most of the journey home and once again, Keira chatted virtually non-stop and Nick didn't seem to tire of her endless talk, not once. She was particularly happy with the huge toy penguin that Nick had bought her, which needed Emma's and Rose's laps as well as Keira's for the journey home.

They arrived back in the village in the early evening and Rose immediately invited them all in for coffee. Emma wished she hadn't, particularly when Nick and John both seemed so keen. In some ways she didn't want the day to end, while in others she just wished it was over. Now she'd seen how Keira was with Nick, she knew she'd be okay with him on her own if ever he wanted to take her out for the day. And him not wanting to take her out for the day was just about as unthinkable as Emma giving her up altogether.

'I'm bushed,' John said with a yawn. 'But I'd love a coffee and a chance to stretch my legs a little.'

'I really don't think . . . ' Emma began.

'Neither do I,' Rose interrupted. 'So why don't you and Nick go down to the pub and have a drink while we stay here, and John can get to know Keira a little better? We've hardly seen her all day. It's a lovely evening. We can sit out in the garden for a while.'

'But you were the ones who . . . ' Emma tried again, but Rose hushed her with a flick of her neatly arched eyebrows.

'Do you enjoy gardening, John?' Rose turned to Nick's father, effectively dismissing Emma from the conversation.

'I do indeed,' John said.

As they walked down the path, Keira slipped her hand into John's. 'I've got my own little garden, Grandpa,' she said, then stifled a yawn with her small hand. 'I plant it all myself and I water it and put special food down to help my flowers grow.'

'Well that sounds wonderful, darling,' John said. 'I'd love to see it. Will you show me?'

★ ★ ★

'You go on ahead,' Nick said. 'I'll catch up with you.'

'Why?'

'Something I want to say to Rose,' he said. 'Please. Humour me.'

He waited until Emma had gone before calling Rose back. For a moment they both watched his father and daughter looking at the child's little section of the garden.

'Please, Nick,' Rose said. 'Don't say any more. Not now. Not today. I know you hate me and you have every right to be angry.'

'Yes,' he said. 'I am angry. Angry with myself. I'm sorry, Rose. When I saw Keira it all hit me so hard, what I'd missed, and I took it out on you. It was wrong. We've all made mistakes, but this isn't the time to dwell on the past, is it? The future is right there — our future.' He nodded towards Keira. 'And for the record, I don't hate you. How could I hate the person who has taken such good care of Emma and Keira? I promise I will never take her and Emma away from you. There's been enough hurt. Will you forgive me, Rose?'

She almost knocked him over when she flung her arms round him. He hugged her back, the last dregs of his anger and bitterness finally fading away.

'Now go,' she said, pushing him away. 'Go to Emma. We've made things right between us; now make things right with Emma, Nick.'

'I know just what she's up to,' Emma fumed as Nick ran to catch up with her.

'Oh yes, and what would that be exactly?'

'Well . . . ' Emma turned to face him. 'Pushing us together like this, sending us out for a drink, treating us as if were . . . were . . . '

'Were a couple,' Nick finished for her. 'Needing a break from the family and time to ourselves.'

'Exactly,' Emma said crossly, because she was terrified that Nick would be

301

frightened off. 'And I'll have words with her later, I can promise you that. The only reason my aunt wanted to come along was to keep your father occupied. The last thing I want right now is . . . ' She took a deep breath. 'Why are you looking at me like that?'

'Like what?'

'That!' She wished he wouldn't look at her so deeply, so intensely. It took her breath away, and she needed all the oxygen she could get right now. 'The last thing I want is for you to feel under any kind of pressure. This is strictly no strings, Nick. Just because you are going to be a part of Keira's life — and I hope a very big part — I don't want you to think that you are in any way obligated to me.'

'Did I tell you you looked beautiful today?' he asked, cutting her off right in the middle of her big, important speech.

'What?'

'You look beautiful,' he said. 'Oh hell, Emma, I can't do this anymore. I can't

302

stop the way I feel about you and I can't keep hiding it. I know what you're saying, but hasn't it sunk in yet? I love you! Love you from the depths of my soul, and nothing is going to change the way I feel.'

They stood facing each other on the empty path in the quiet village with the dusky evening light swirling around them in a misty haze. Had he really just said what she thought he had?

'You still feel . . . ' she stammered. 'After everything, you still . . . '

'Love you? More than ever,' he said and he reached out suddenly, grabbed her hands and pulled her towards him so hard that she fell against him. 'Especially when you throw yourself at me like that.'

'I didn't!' She began to struggle, then stopped suddenly.

Why was she struggling? Why was she trying to deny how she felt? It suddenly dawned on her that there was nothing to keep them apart anymore. He knew about her secret babies and he loved her more than ever. He didn't hold it against her, didn't hate her, wasn't angry with her. They'd found peace and more, so much more. Too much time had been wasted already. She wasn't going to waste any more.

'Oh, Nick,' she whispered and lifted her hands to his head, winding her fingers in his hair and pulling his face down to hers. They kissed lightly, their lips barely touching, but it was like touching a match to a fuse.

They might have been the only two people left in the world. Everything about this felt so right.

'Have I convinced you that I love you?' he asked her at last, his eyes searching hers. 'Do you believe me now?'

'Yes. And I love you too, Nick.'

'You know where we go from here, don't you?' he asked, his voice tender.

'To the pub?' she said with a mischievous smile.

'To forever,' he said. 'You and me and Keira. But first, yes, we'd better go to the pub. We have a lot to talk about.'

* * *

It was dark and getting cooler as they made their way home. Stars twinkled in the sky above them. The air was so clean and sweet-smelling, the canopy of the sky so beautiful above them, the world suddenly such a wonderful, wonderful place.

Nick stopped suddenly and turned, pulling Emma into his arms. 'We have such a lot of time to make up,' he said.

'I know,' she whispered against his chest.

'And Keira! She's just amazing,' he went on. 'I love her so much already, can you believe that?'

'Of course I can.' She laughed softly. 'She's a very lovable child.'

'No, it's more than that. She's my child. Ours. Yours and mine. We made her, Emma; our love created her. Because we were in love, weren't we?'

'I think I remember the very night she was conceived,' Emma admitted for the first time. 'It was a very special night. It was the night I realised just how much I loved you.'

He closed his eyes and kissed the top of her head. 'And I let you go, in my stupidity and arrogance.'

'You weren't stupid or arrogant,' she said. 'We were both young and impulsive. We both made mistakes, but fate has given us a second chance.'

He grinned at her. 'Come on, let's get back. Keira has to go to bed and I don't want Dad to be late to bed either. It's been quite a day.'

They walked slowly back to the cottage, arms around each other, reluctant to let even air come between them.

When they reached home, they stopped at the same moment. The cottages had warm, welcoming lights in the windows and the air was still and peaceful.

'Will you marry me, Emma?' Nick whispered. 'Soon?'

She knew she should think about it, but she didn't have to.

'Yes, oh yes,' she said.

It was the following spring when Emma and Nick emerged from the village church into a shower of rose petals thrown in the air by Keira, who had never looked prettier than she did today in a deep red dress with a tiara of white rosebuds in her hair that matched the white roses Emma carried.

Among the guests were Jenny and Scott with their beautiful twins, James and Edward. And Melanie was there with her parents Nat and Doreen and her little girl, Paige. In fact many of the guests were parents with the babies Emma and Nick had delivered, and staff from the hospital.

They posed for photographs in front of the beautiful church and as they made their way to the village pub where they were holding the reception, Emma realised that Keira wasn't with them.

'I know where she'll be,' Nick murmured. 'Dad, Rose, you go on ahead to the reception, and make sure everyone has a drink. We'll be along in a while.'

Holding tightly to Emma's hand, he led her back to the church, this time entering through the little wooden gate to the side. And there was Keira, sitting on the grass beside her sister's grave.

It should have been a heart-wrenching moment, a moment of sadness and sorrow, but Keira had arranged her bridesmaid's posy in the vase and was telling Daisy all about their father as she tied the white ribbon from her flowers around the vase.

'Mummy's so happy,' she said. 'And Daddy is so handsome and kind. We're going to stay here forever now so we'll always be near you, Daisy.'

'Oh, Nick,' Emma whispered and he squeezed her hand.

'We have a lovely grandpa too,' Keira went on. 'He makes me laugh and he buys me sweeties and tells me not to tell Mummy or Daddy, but he says that's what grandpas are for.'

She sensed their presence and turned round, smiling all over her face.

'Mummy! Daddy!' she cried, jumping to her feet and rushing into their waiting arms. 'Is it time to go?'

'Yes, sweetheart,' Nick said, and Emma felt perilously close to tears. But if any tears fell today, they would be tears of happiness — for now their family was united and strong, nothing would ever come between them again.

THE END

We do hope that you have enjoyed reading this large print book.

Did you know that all of our titles are available for purchase?

We publish a wide range of high quality large print books including:
Romances, Mysteries, Classics
General Fiction
Non Fiction and Westerns

Special interest titles available in large print are:
The Little Oxford Dictionary
Music Book, Song Book
Hymn Book, Service Book

Also available from us courtesy of Oxford University Press:
Young Readers' Dictionary
(large print edition)
Young Readers' Thesaurus
(large print edition)

For further information or a free brochure, please contact us at:
Ulverscroft Large Print Books Ltd.,
The Green, Bradgate Road, Anstey,
Leicester, LE7 7FU, England.
Tel: (00 44) **0116 236 4325**
Fax: (00 44) **0116 234 0205**

WHISPERS ON THE PLAINS

Noelene Jenkinson

Widowed wheat farmer Dusty Nash, of Sunday Plains pastoral station, is captivated by the spirited redhead who arrives in the district. Irish teacher Meghan Dorney has left her floundering engagement for a six-month posting to the outback of Western Australia. Thrown together in the small, isolated community, each resists their budding attraction to resolve personal issues and tragedy. But when Dusty learns the truth about the newcomer, can he forgive enough to love?

SUZI LEARNS TO LOVE AGAIN

Patricia Keyson

Upon meeting troublesome pupil Tom's father, Cameron, young schoolteacher Suzi feels an immediate attraction. She is determined not to be drawn into a relationship, knowing she would feel unfaithful to her late husband; but the more time Cameron and Suzi spend together, the more they are captivated by each other. Suzi rediscovers deep emotions, though she agrees with Cameron that Tom must come first . . . But how long can Suzi hide her love for Cameron?

THE DUKE & THE VICAR'S DAUGHTER

Fenella J. Miller

The Duke of Edbury decides he must marry an heiress if he is to save his estates. So far he has managed to stay out of the clutches of the predatory mothers who spend the Season searching for suitable husbands for their daughters. The god-daughter of his aunt, Lady Patience, might be a suitable candidate, and he is persuaded to act as a temporary guardian to both her and her cousin, Charity Lawson. When Charity and Patience exchange places, the fun begins . . .

A PLACE OF PEACE

Sally Quilford

When Nell participates in a transatlantic house-swap, going to stay in New England on the beautiful Barratt Island for three months, she hopes to escape the shame she left behind in Derbyshire. She soon meets gorgeous police chief Colm Barratt — and scheming socialite Julia Silkwood, whose husband's health seems to be failing suspiciously quickly. With Nell's overactive imagination running riot, and her past about to catch up with her, she fears she could lose Colm forever.